WHERE HIGHWAYS CROSS

WHERE HIGHWAYS CROSS

J.S. FLETCHER

BROWNSTONE BOOKS

Originally pubished in 1895.

PART THE FIRST

INTRODUCTION

Joseph Smith Fletcher (1863–1935) was an English journalist and author. He wrote more than 230 books on a wide variety of subjects, both fiction and non-fiction, and was one of the most prolific English writers of detective fiction—the work for which he is chiefly remembered today.

Fletcher was born in Halifax, West Yorkshire, the son of a clergyman. His father died when he was eight months old, and his grandmother took him in and raised him on a farm in Darrington, near Pontefract, in Yorkshire. He was educated at Silcoates School in Wakefield, and after some study of law, became a journalist at age 20.

He started work as a sub-editor in London, but soon returned to Yorkshire, where he worked first on the Leeds *Mercury* using the pseudonym "A Son of the Soil," and then as a special correspondent for the *Yorkshire Post*. Among other things, he covered Edward VII's coronation in 1902.

Fletcher's first books published were poetry. He then wrote numerous, and now largely forgotten, works of historical fiction and history, many dealing with Yorkshire. His regional work led to his selection as a fellow of the Royal Historical Society.

Michael Sadleir stated that Fletcher's historical novel, *When Charles I Was King* (1892), was his best work. Fletcher wrote several novels of rural life in imitation of Richard Jefferies, beginning with *The Wonderful Wapentake* (1894), but it wasn't until 1914, when Fletcher wrote his first detective novel, that he truly found his calling.

Over the last two decates of his life, he went on to write over a hundred more mysteries, many featuring the private investigator Ronald Camberwell.

Fletcher is sometimes incorrectly described as a "Golden Age of Detective Fiction" author, but he is in fact an almost exact contemporary of Arthur Conan Doyle, the creator of Sherlock Holmes. The bulk of his detective fiction works considerably pre-date the period considered the Golden Age, and even those few published within it do not conform to the closed form and strict rules professed, if not unfailingly observed, by Golden Age writers.

His work is still enjoyable today. Although some volumes have mildly racist elements, as were common in fiction of the era, the modern reader should keep in mind the period in which they were originally published.

—Karl Wurf
Rockville, Maryland

CHAPTER I
THE STATUTE HIRING FAIR

Outside the town of Sicaster, going north-by-north-west, the high-road leads through a somewhat level country, mainly concerned with coal-mining, towards the great city of Clothford, thirteen miles away. On this side of Sicaster the land has few features of interest or beauty. Here and there stands an ancient mansion, embowered in trees and shielded from contact with the unlovely colliery villages by carefully-fenced parks and enclosures. In the villages themselves the observant traveller often finds traces of old houses which were no doubt picturesque and countrified in the days when agriculture was preferred to coal-mining. The greater part of the district, however, is somewhat dingy and dark, and the lover of nature sees little to admire in it. But within two miles of Sicaster the scenery shows signs of change for the better. The high-road becomes suddenly straight, and, leaving the coal-district in the rear, runs along the side of Sicaster Park, a vast enclosure where race-meetings are held twice a year. It rises a little at this point, and in the far distance stands Sicaster itself, a mass of red roofs and grey walls, with the quaint steeple of St. Giles's Church overtopping the irregular gables and chimneys. Beyond Sicaster there are no more coal-mines. The town once passed, the traveller sees before him the long, rolling meadows and wide cornfields which make Osgoldcross one of the most fertile and beautiful divisions of Yorkshire.

Along that portion of the high-road which runs parallel with Sicaster Park there walked, one November afternoon, some twenty years ago, a woman who was obviously wearied to the verge of extreme fatigue. The day was cold and slightly wet. A thin, intermittent rain came with the gusts of wind that blew fitfully across the park, and the woman, as she walked on, drew her shawl more closely about her shoulders, as if to protect herself from the weather. Coming to one of the bridle-gates opening into the park, she paused and leaned against it. A waggon, drawn by two stout horses, was following her from the direction of Clothford, and she looked back along the road and watched it draw nearer. The waggoner whistled as he came along, and his merry tune was accompanied by the jingle of the brass bells that hung from the head-gear of his horses. As he came abreast of her he cast his eye on the woman by the wayside.

"Will you ride in, missis?" he called across the road. "'Tisn't far, but it's better riding than walking to-day."

The woman looked at him doubtfully for a moment, and then, persuaded by his cheery face, or coaxed by the comparative luxury of the canvas-topped tilt under which he sat, she crossed the road with a word of thanks. The waggoner pulled up his team with a jerk, gave her a hand, and helped her to a seat at his side.

"You are very kind," she said. "I am tired."

"Aye, I daresay, missis," he answered. "T' road's wet, and bad for walking."

He started his horses again with a chirruping sound from his pursed-up mouth. The road began to rise thereabouts, and they went slowly. The waggoner resumed his whistling, but twisted his head round to take stock of his companion. At the first sight of her, resting against the bridle-gate, he took her for a tramp, but when she crossed the road and faced him he saw that he had been mistaken. He now saw, on such examination as he could make by surreptitious glances out of his eye-corners, that she was neatly if scantily attired in garments that had obviously been good and of somewhat fashionable style, and that her whole appearance showed unmistakable traces of personal care. She wore gloves and a veil, and beneath the latter the waggoner saw a face that was young and attractive, with delicate features and pathetic eyes, and a mouth that drooped a little at the corners as if with anxiety or grief. He whistled more softly on making these discoveries, but his companion apparently took no heed of the music which he made. Her eyes were fixed on the red roofs that shut in the vanishing point of the long, straight high-road; her hands lay in her lap, the fingers lacing and interlacing each other.

"Nasty day," said the waggoner at length. "Both for man and beast, as the saying is."

The woman half turned towards him. Something in the movement suggested to him that she had until then forgotten his presence.

"Yes," she answered. She turned from him again, and looked once more along the road. "What place is that we're coming to?" she enquired.

"That, missis? That's Sicaster."

She gave a little sigh of relief.

"I'm glad of that," she said. "It's a long way from Clothford, isn't it, when you walk all the way?"

"On such a day as this, missis, why, yes, it is," answered the waggoner. "A long way indeed."

He cast further glances at her from his eye-corners, and being of an inquisitive nature, would have liked to ask her why she had walked, seeing that the railway was near and trains were plentiful. The woman, however, showed no further disposition to talk, and he took to whistling again and stirred his horses into a slow trot.

The road now crossed a railway bridge, and after dipping slightly, began to ascend through rows of ancient houses towards the heart of the town. The horses slowed down their pace, and as the jangling noise of their bells became fainter, the waggoner and his companion became aware of the sound of such harsh music as may be made by the beating of drums and cymbals and the blowing of horns and trumpets.

"What's that?" asked the woman.

"It's the stattits, missis," said the waggoner. "Sicaster stattits, and that's the music of the shows and the wild beasts and such like."

"What are the stattits?"

"Lord love us, why, the stattits is when all the country-folk come to be hired! There's rare doings in the Market-Place, I'll lay a penny. Fat women, and real giants, and men turned to stone, and such things as them. But here we are at the *Cross-Keys*, and I'm going no further at present, missis," said the waggoner.

He helped his companion to alight at the door of a little inn which stood at the entrance to a large open space filled at that moment by a bustling throng of people who elbowed and jostled each other as they moved from one show to another. The woman stood on the pavement and looked somewhat helplessly about her. The waggoner tied up his reins to the cart-head, keeping his eye on her the while.

"Can you tell me where the Market-Place is?" she asked him. "I want to find somebody there, and I've never been here before."

"You can't miss it, missis," answered the waggoner. "Go straight down—there past the shows—that's the Corn-market—and through the Beast-fair—and there you are in the Market-Place."

The woman thanked him for his kindness, and went away in the direction of the noisy crowd. In the Corn-market every available inch of space was occupied by the shows and the people thronging about them. One side of the square was filled up by a menagerie of wild animals. On the platform outside it sat the bandsmen whose drums and trumpets made blaring music that failed to drown the roaring and shrill cries of the beasts inside the vans. The people crowded with a steady persistence up the steps leading to the entrance. Those who had already been inside and who had emerged with faces expressive of wonder, grouped themselves about the entrances of smaller shows, one of which held a wild man, and another a lamb with three heads. Outside each of these frail erections of sail-cloth and canvas there stood a barrel-organ or a gong, and these being continuously ground or beaten, added fresh discord to the babel of sound that arose on all sides. The whole scene was one of noise and hubbub, of jostling and horse-play, and the blowing of the trumpets and beating of the gongs tended to produce a feeling of confusion in anyone who had not previously attended similar gatherings.

The young woman who had ridden into the town with the friendly waggoner made her way along the skirts of the crowd until she came to the Market-Place. Here the scene was even noisier and more perplexing than in the wider Corn-market, for the pavement was lined with stalls at which small hucksters sold sweet-stuffs and cheap commodities, and the space beyond was filled with more shows, roundabouts, and canvas booths. Here, also, the people were more crowded together and seemed to be waiting for something to happen. A row of farm-labourers, some of whom carried whips in their hands, stood on the curb; a crowd of young women, dressed in their best, sheltered under the low roof of the old Butter-Cross. Farmers in stout driving coats and leggings walked about in the throng or chatted in groups at the shop-doors, while young folks and children clustered about the stalls or pushed their way to the fronts of the shows. Arrived there they stood in open-mouthed admiration of the gorgeous paintings that placarded the wonders to be seen inside. At all these things the stranger scarcely looked; her eyes were busily engaged in studying the signs over the shop-doors in the Market-Place. She went along one side of it without finding what she wanted, which was a dressmaker's establishment in which there was a vacant situation that she had hopes of filling. She found it at length on the direction of a friendly countrywoman, but diffidence or anxiety prevented her from entering it for a moment or two. At last she summoned sufficient courage to open the door and walk into the shop. She came out again in a few minutes with disappointment visibly expressed on her pale face. The vacant situation had been filled up that morning.

The young woman withdrew from the crowd into a quiet alley opening out of the Market-Place, and after making sure that she was unobserved, drew out a shabby leather purse from her pocket and examined the contents. Upon counting the coppers which it contained she found that she had but tenpence. She replaced the purse, and went back into the Market-Place, feeling sick at heart. She had walked from Clothford in the hope of getting the situation for which she had just made application, and her errand being fruitless, she was now in a difficult position.

Wandering aimlessly through the throng she came along the north side of the Market-Place until she reached the Butter-Cross. Here she stood looking hopelessly about her until her attention was arrested by the group of girls and young women who stood on the steps of the Cross, laughing and talking together. She noticed that now and then a farmer and his wife would step up to one or other of these and hold a conversation which seemed to partake of the nature of a bargain. Out of sheer curiosity the stranger enquired of a woman what the girls stood there for. The woman regarded her curiously.

"Why, to be hired, of course," she answered. "They're looking out for situations, and they're mighty particular, too, some on 'em, for servants are scarce to-day."

The stranger hesitated a moment, and then she made her way through the throng and took her place on the Butter-Cross.

CHAPTER II
THE FASTENING PENNY

The young women on the Butter-Cross looked at the new-comer with something of wonder and disdain. She was obviously not of their own class, nor fitted for the work which domestic servants are expected to perform in farm-houses. Her pale face and retiring air formed a marked contrast to their own ruddy countenances and confident demeanour. They began to whisper amongst themselves, glancing at the stranger with eyes which were not altogether friendly. She, however, took no notice of them, but stood waiting for someone to accost her. The farmers and their wives, who came into the Cross and looked about them, gazed at her curiously, but did not speak to her. The men wondered who she was, and what she did there; the women, keener in their criticism, decided that all was not well with her. Being somewhat dulled by the disappointment she had just experienced, the stranger did not perceive the effect her presence had produced. Her attitude was one of apathetic expectation; she merely waited to see if anything would happen.

After a time there advanced through the constantly-moving throng a man who paused for a moment at the foot of the steps leading to the Butter-Cross, and looked upward at the people above. He was a tall, broad-shouldered person of apparently forty years of age, dressed in a long grey driving coat which came nearly to his feet, but left a glimpse of his stout leather gaiters. His clean-shaven face was dark and full of character. His eyes were somewhat deep-set in his head, and his mouth, which was full and firm, gave the impression of a strong will that was further deepened by his square jaw and bold chin. He seemed to be of a somewhat superior class to most of the men standing by, and some of these greeted him in passing with more show of respect than they made towards their fellows.

The new-comer glanced at the crowd within the Butter-Cross without any particular sign of interest until his eye fell on the young woman who had just taken up her station there. She still stood looking out upon the throng, apparently taking little notice of what was going on around her. Her appearance showed him that she was a stranger to the place and the people, her indifference to her surroundings told him that she was not of the class of girls who usually offer themselves for domestic service in farm-houses. As she had not seen him, or betrayed no sign of having done so, he felt no compunction in continuing to gaze at her and to study her face, which seemed to him to be a singularly attractive one. Presently he mounted the steps and mixed with the throng. Some of the girls knew him and replied respectfully to his greeting. He walked in and out between them, but after a while returned to the stranger and addressed her.

"Are you looking for a situation?" he said.

The young woman started as if from a reverie and looked at her questioner. The man was regarding her intently, but with a certain kindliness in his eyes which made her reply to him with some confidence.

"I should be thankful for one, sir," she answered.

"I am wanting someone," he said, and stopped short as if not sure of what he was about to say. "Have you any experience of domestic service?" he enquired, after a pause.

A little spot of colour came into the girl's cheeks. The man noticed it quickly, and spoke again before she could answer him.

"I mean of household requirements," he said. "I don't want servants so much as someone who could give them a sort of superintendence. Do you know anything of baking, now, or sewing?"

"I know plenty about sewing, sir."

"Ah, you've perhaps been engaged in that sort of work?"

"Yes, sir."

He looked at her curiously, tapping his boot with the ash stick which he carried in his hand, and obviously disliking to put personal questions to her. The young woman, however, found courage to relieve his embarrassment.

"I was engaged in the dressmaking business at Clothford," she said, "but my mistress failed in business, and I could not find another situation there. I heard of a place here at Sicaster, so I walked over to apply for it to-day, but it was filled up when I got here."

"You walked over from Clothford? That's a long distance on such a nasty day. Why didn't you take the train?"

"Because I couldn't afford it, sir."

"I see—I see. I'm sorry I asked that—I didn't think what I was saying. Now about this business of mine—I'm a farmer, and I have a strong servant who does all the actual work, but I want someone to see after things a little—not exactly a housekeeper, you know, but somebody that could mend and sew, and keep my rooms tidy, and see that things were as they ought to be. What do you think? Could you undertake that?"

"I think so, sir. I've kept house—and I am tidy and orderly, I believe."

16

"That I can see. Well, I think we might arrange. You see, I don't want a young woman such as these behind us. I want something superior—somebody that has a bit of better feeling and knows how things should be done. The setting of a table for dinner, now—could you see to that?"

"Oh yes, sir."

"And such things as choosing curtains for a parlour, now, or making linen for the house—you could manage all that, I daresay?"

"I'm sure I could, sir."

"That's what I want. My old servant—she's been with me a long time—is very good at plain cooking and at kitchen work, but of course she doesn't pretend to more. Well, now, what would you say about wages—I haven't much idea myself."

"I don't know, sir. Perhaps I ought to tell you that I was never used to—to this, until recently. But I have no friends, and my husband is—is dead—"

"Yes, yes," said the man. "Don't cry—it comes to all of us—but it's hard, no doubt."

"And so I had to earn my own living after that," said the young woman, making a resolute attempt to keep back her tears, "and dressmaking was all that I could do, and lately—"

"I understand. Well, now, what would you say to your board and lodging and fifteen pounds a year? That was what I reckoned to pay for the service I want."

"I should be glad of it, sir, for I am practically destitute. I would do my best to earn it."

"Well, I'm sure you would. Perhaps you could give me the name of the dressmaker you worked for in Clothford for a reference. It's the usual thing to do so, though I suppose it's fast a form."

"Oh, yes, sir. It was Mrs. Feather, in Widegate—though, of coarse, the shop is closed now."

"I know the name. Well, now, we'll call our bargain settled then, and I hope you'll try to do what I want. My old servant's a little bit touchy, but I daresay you won't disagree with her. Now, what's your name?"

"Elisabeth Verrell, sir."

"Very well, Elisabeth—I'll write it down in my pocket-book. My name is Hepworth—Thorndyke Hepworth—and if you'd like to ask any questions about me, anybody in the fair will answer them, or any of the Sicaster shopkeepers. Well, now, let me see—oh, there's one thing I mustn't forget."

He unbuttoned his long coat and drew forth a leather bag from his breeches' pocket. From this he extracted a half-sovereign, and held it towards Elisabeth. She looked at it in astonishment.

"What's that for, sir?"

Hepworth smiled.

"I forgot," said he. "Of course, if you're a stranger hereabouts you don't know the custom. That's a fastening penny to conclude the bargain. Now, you'll perhaps be wanting some little thing before I drive home, and if I were you, as it's a cold day, I'd go and have something to eat—there's a good eating-house close by—and oh, you'll be having a box to take, perhaps?"

"No, sir—my box is at Clothford—I must send for it."

"Very good, Elisabeth. Then go, get your tea, and meet me at the Elephant Hotel at six o'clock—ask the ostler for Mr. Hepworth's conveyance."

Hepworth now turned away and went down the steps of the Cross into the Market-Place, where he was presently lost to sight amongst the crowd. Elisabeth watched him wonderingly until he disappeared. She was a little confused at the sudden change in her fortune, and was inclined to ponder over it. She recognised friendliness in the way Hepworth had spoken to her. She had been so lonely and sick at heart until he addressed her that a certain numbness of spirit had filled her mind and made her insensible to much of what was going on around her. Now that there was some definite prospect of gaining an honest living presented to her, her spirits revived, and she left the Butter-Cross with a lighter heart.

Elisabeth made her way to the eating-house which Hepworth had pointed out. She had not tasted food for many hours, and her breakfast, taken at Clothford, had been of poor and unsubstantial quality. She now felt keenly hungry, and entered the eating-house with something like alacrity. The place was well patronised: there were few vacant corners, but she found one near the door and slipped into it. The young woman who waited on customers came to her and recommended her to try ham-and-eggs. The house, she said, was famous for its ham-and-eggs, and the price was moderate. Elisabeth acquiesced: she was famishing, and could have eaten anything that the waitress chose to set before her.

While Elisabeth was enjoying her meal, one of the girls who had stood near her on the Butter-Cross came in and took a seat at the same table. She was a plain-faced country girl, with a kindly expression of countenance, and she had been almost the only one of the crowd not to talk or giggle over the stranger's appearance. She now looked at Elisabeth with a new interest, and presently addressed her.

"I see'd you talking to Mr. Hepworth," she said. "Perhaps you're going to place there. You'll excuse me for speaking, but I used to live there myself once."

Elisabeth saw that there was no undue inquisitiveness in the girl's manner. She replied that she was going to service at Mr. Hepworth's, as the girl supposed.

"And a rare good master he is," said the girl, with emphasis. "I should ha' liked to stay there, but he had one servant already, old Mally, and besides, I had a bad illness. I expect you'll be going as a sort o' parlour maid—he's a very gentleman-like sort o' man, is Mr. Hepworth, and likes things doing right. He's a religious man, too: he preaches at the Chapel sometimes. He was very good to me when I was badly—used to read to me for an hour at a time, and buy me things to do me good. I don't think nobody could find a better place than that. I'm stopping again in my present place, and I wish I wasn't."

Elisabeth heard this news with considerable satisfaction, and was not averse to hearing more. But as it was by that time drawing near to six o'clock, and as she had yet to enquire her way to the Elephant Hotel, she said good-afternoon and went away.

CHAPTER III
THE HOME FARM

When Elisabeth entered the inn-yard she found Hepworth waiting for her. His horse was already yoked to the gig, and he himself was superintending the bestowal of various parcels under the seat. He assisted Elisabeth to climb into the gig, and gave her a rug to wrap about her knees before he got in beside her. Then he drove out of the yard by a back way that escaped the noise and bustle of the fair, and presently turned into a road that led away from Sicaster in the opposite direction to that by which Elisabeth had entered the town. By that time the light rain that had fallen with more or less persistency during the afternoon had ceased, and given place to a clear evening and a starlit sky. Elisabeth, unused to riding at a rapid pace in an open conveyance, shivered a little as the gig emerged upon the unsheltered road.

"You'll feel the cold, I daresay," said Hepworth. "I'm used to it, and it makes no difference to me. Now, there's a spare rug behind—how would it be if you put it about your shoulders?"

He pulled up the horse as he spoke, and reaching the rug from the back seat, assisted his companion in somewhat clumsy fashion, as if he were not used to the task, to wrap herself in it. Elisabeth thanked him, and was glad of the rug—the cold was keen, and her garments were ill-fitted to withstand it.

Hepworth drove on through the darkness, speaking little to Elisabeth, save to enquire now and then if she felt the cold. They passed through a village, the windows of which showed faint gleams of lamp-light, and went onward along a bleak portion of the road over which an ancient corn-mill, faintly defined against the dark sky, stood sentry-like. Then came another village, larger and more straggling than the first, a mere collection of lamp-lighted windows seen fitfully in the darkness. When it was passed the road dipped into a country thickly covered by deep woods, the tree-tops of which showed in tremulous shapes against the sky. Suddenly the horse turned out of the highway into a narrow lane, shadowed on one side by the wood, and after following this for a hundred yards or so, stopped at a gate. Hepworth handed the reins to Elisabeth, and got down from the gig. Having led the horse through the gate and closed it behind them, he regained his seat, and drove forward at a walking pace. Elisabeth perceived that they were traversing the outside of a paddock thickly planted with huge trees whose branches swept the ground. Presently the lights of the house shone out through the darkness, and the gig stopped at the gate of the fold. The kitchen door opened, and a broad stream of light revealed the figures of a man carrying a lantern, and of a woman who stood behind him in the doorway. Hepworth got down from the gig, and assisted Elisabeth to alight. She stood waiting while he gave some directions to the man as to the disposal of the horse. At his bidding she then followed her new master into the kitchen. A middle-aged woman of a somewhat grim, but not unpleasant countenance, stood by the great fireplace when they entered, evidently superintending certain cooking operations which gave forth an inviting odour. She looked questioningly from Hepworth to Elisabeth.

"Now, Mally," said Hepworth. "I've found a young woman to do the bit of work we talked about. Elisabeth's her name—I'm sure you'll get on together. I daresay you'll tell her all that she wants to know, but she'll be tired to-night, so we won't ask her to do anything."

"There's nowt to do," said Mally, triumphantly. She looked at Elisabeth, and nodded. "Sit you down, lass—come to the fire. I lay it's cowd as Christmas outside, and drivin's a cowd job at t' best o' times. Now maister, if you'll nobbut go into t' parlour, I'll see 'at all's reight—I can't do wi' men about me when I'm busy."

Hepworth laughed, and disappeared into the parlour through a double door. Mally presently carried there a tray loaded with food, and shut the inner door behind her. Elisabeth heard her voice and Hepworth's in conversation. She looked round her. The kitchen in which she sat was a pattern of tidiness. The big table in the side window-place had been scrubbed to the whiteness of snow; the hearthstone was elaborately decorated with designs in potter-mould; the brass candlesticks on the mantelpiece shone like burnished gold. Elisabeth, strange as the place was to her, felt a sense of peace and security in these evidences of the old servant's orderliness.

Mally presently returned from the parlour, again closing both the doors behind her. She approached Elisabeth, and laid her hand not unkindly upon the young woman's shoulder.

"Your jacket's damp, my lass," said she. "Off wi' it, and hang it up ower th' hearthstone. You shall hev' a drop o' tea, scaldin' hot, to tak' the cowd out o' you."

Elisabeth protested that she had already had tea at Sicaster, but she hastened to follow Mally's advice as to the jacket.

"A drop o' good tea, made as I mak' it," said Mally, "weern't

22

hurt nobody. Down wi' it, lass, while it's hot. If you've hed your tea at Sicaster, you weern't be wantin' owt to ate just now, but happen you'll do wi' a bit o' supper later on. There's no stint in this house for onnybody."

Elisabeth drank the tea which Mally gave her. It was strong and good, and of an infinitely superior taste and quality to that which she had tasted in the Sicaster eating-house. She said as much to Mally, who sat on the opposite side of the hearth, and drank her own tea out of a pint bowl. Mally wagged her head wisely.

"I tak' no notice o' them ateing-houses and their tea," said she. "It's nobbut poor wishy-washy stuff at t' best o' times, and their bread's sad, and t' butter's sour. I'd rather pine thro' here to Sicaster and back, and hev' my own when I get home again, than depend o' them ateing-houses."

She then said that as the master would want nothing for a while, she would show Elisabeth the house, so that she might know her way about next morning. Elisabeth assented with alacrity, and followed Mally through various chambers, upstairs and downstairs, all scrupulously clean and old-fashioned, and redolent of soap and water. Before a great chest on the staircase Mally paused and looked at her companion with a significant expression.

"That'll be your job, lass," she said. "It's linen, is that; sheets, and table-cloths, and napery, and the good Lord knows what. The maister's mother bowt it, and took great store in it, but it hevn't been so well seen to sin' she were takken, poor thing. I've a deal to do wi' the cookin', and there's three men in the house besides the maister, and I can't pretend to be much of a hand at gettin' things up, and layin' tables with napkins and so on. You'll be able to do that, I des'say." Elisabeth answered that she thought she would.

"The maister," said Mally, "is a very particular man about them things, and he's gotten more so lately. You see, he's a great reader, and he's high-larnt, and keeps very good company, and when he has onnybody here he likes his table to look smart. And, Lord love ye, I don't know nowt about layin' a table wi' napkins and things, but I hope you do, my lass, I'm sure."

"I think I can manage all that," said Elisabeth, secretly amused at the old servant's confession.

"Well, lass, well, I'll answer for the cookin', and that's the main part, to my mind," said Mally. "Better a bare board and plenty to eat, than a fine table wi' nowt on it."

With this wise remark she led the way downstairs and along a passage to a back-kitchen, in which the three men-servants to whom

23

she had referred sat round a roaring wood fire. One of them had just returned from the statute-hiring fair, and had brought back with him a song-paper, the contents of which he was singing over to his companions. All three stared hard at Elisabeth.

"Now, then," said Mally, "that's Bill, and this is Tom, and yon's Reuben. They can all ate like sojers on a march, and they keep me bakin' every day. Reuben, hes ta filled t' boiler?"

"Aye," said Reuben. "Long sin'."

"And hes ta locked t' hen-hoil door, and browt t' kay in?"

"Aye—aboon an hour agoöa."

"Well, there'll be a hot tatie for all on ye at supper-time—if ye're good lads, mind," said Mally, retiring with Elisabeth. "I hev' to give 'em a bit of a treat, you know, lass," she said apologetically, as they went back to the front-kitchen. "'Cos they do little jobs for me now and then. You can do owt wi' men if ye nobbut fill their bellies."

At nine o'clock, Mally and Elisabeth having washed up the tea-things which the former fetched from the parlour, Mally called the three men into the front-kitchen, where they sat on a bench against the wall in an attitude that suggested schoolboy-like attention. Elisabeth wondered what this might mean, and was still more mystified when Mally knocked loudly at the parlour door, and cried, "All ready, maister!" In response to her summons Hepworth presently appeared, carrying a huge Bible. He laid it on the table in the centre of the kitchen, and opening it, read a chapter from the New Testament. Elisabeth, who had never been present at such a service, listened curiously as he read. He had a full, deep voice, and read with some artistic perception, and the three men on the kitchen bench seemed to enjoy the reading, and kept their eyes fixed on their master's face. As soon as the chapter was finished Hepworth closed the book and stood up. The three men said, "Good-night, maister," and stamped away down the passage.

"Now, Mally," said Hepworth, coming over to the fireside. "You'll see after Elisabeth, I'm sure. You'll know what she'll—"

"Go your ways, maister," said Mally. "Leave women-folk to see to theirsens. Men's nobbut in the way at t' best o' times."

Hepworth laughed, and bidding the two women good-night, went back to his parlour.

"Now, lass," said Mally, "we'll hev' a bit o' supper, and then to bed. 'Early to sleep and early to rise,' you know, and I'm a rare un for getting up wi' the lark."

"I should like to set the table for Mr. Hepworth's breakfast in the morning," said Elisabeth. "What time will he have it?"

"He's up at six, lass, and he's out till seven, and about half-past he's ready and keen," said Mally. "Aye, you can wait on him—it'll tak' a deal off my shoulders." Accordingly, Elisabeth rose early next morning and proceeded to prepare the parlour for her master's breakfast. It was a somewhat old-fashioned and gloomy apartment, sadly in need of a touch of brightness here and there. Elisabeth reduced it to something like homeliness, and laid the breakfast-table with care and taste. She hunted out a fine linen-cloth, and going out into the garden cut a bunch of chrysanthemums and arranged them in a china bowl in the centre of the table. This done, she borrowed a clean white apron from Mally, and looked very neat and smart when she carried Hepworth's breakfast into the parlour. Hepworth smiled approval.

"That looks very nice, Elisabeth," said he. "I see you know one part of your duties, at any rate."

CHAPTER IV
HEPWORTH

In the eyes of most people thereabouts Hepworth was a man of some peculiarity. He had now reached the age of forty years, and was known to be well-to-do even to the verge of affluence, and yet he had never shown any desire to marry and settle down after the accustomed fashion of country folk. While his mother lived there had been excuses found for him. It was said that he was such a good son that he would not share his devotion between her and a wife. Certainly he devoted himself to her with a constancy and affection that was rare. She was an invalid for many years before her death, and in Hepworth she found a tender nurse. In him, so far as she was concerned, were united feminine gentleness and masculine pity. The country folk made his devotion a proverb, and thought well of him for the manifesting of qualities which are always esteemed by people who are chiefly influenced by their natural environment, and who accordingly esteem the domestic virtues at a high standard. When the old mother died, however, it was usually supposed that Hepworth would soon give a new mistress to the Home Farm. Certainly he had never shown any partiality for any particular person of the opposite sex, and there was therefore no one's name that could be coupled with his own. Young women there were plenty, a Jane here, and a Susan there, who would make excellent wives for a farmer, and it was thought that upon one or other of these he would shortly look with favour. He was at that time but thirty years old—an age which country folk deem a suitable one for marriage—and it seemed unnatural that so prosperous and healthy a man should not take a wife to himself. As the years passed by and he made no sign and showed no liking for female society, it was said that he was taking a long time to pick and choose; now that ten years had gone and he still remained single, some of his neighbours began to think that there was to be neither choosing nor picking, and logically enough they considered his behaviour peculiar. It was not according to tradition, which is the main rule of life amongst a conservative people.

If Hepworth had cared to confess the truth to any of his few friends, he would have told them that he refrained from marriage and even from the thought of marriage for one simple and amply sufficient reason. He had never known what it was to have any feeling of love for woman. Filial affection he knew to its deepest possibilities and would never forget, for he had worshipped his mother as a saint, and retained of her memories and impressions that were nothing short of sacred. But of actual passion, the strong, healthy, not-to-be-resisted desire of man for woman, he knew nothing—there had been nothing in his life so far to call it into existence. From boyhood he had led an active life; at fifteen he was called upon to assist his mother in superintending the affairs of the farm, and it had been necessary for many years that he should not only superintend the labour of others, but also engage in labour with his own hands. He had risen early and worked till sunset, and if he was not then too tired for aught but sleep, he devoted himself to books, for which he had a passion as great as for the brown acres that he tilled. All his life, then, had been devoted to work, to books, and to his mother, and when the companionship of his mother was taken from him, he turned to his books and to his work with renewed zest, finding in them a true and real consolation. One other factor remained in the solitude of his surroundings. In his farmstead he was almost a hermit. One other farm-house and a row of cottages made up with his own house the hamlet in which he lived. There was one village a mile-and-a-half away, and another nearly three miles distant, in which he might have found society had he cared to seek it, but the solitude in which he had mainly lived had exerted its full force on his mind, which was naturally receptive, and as he grew older he found that he was happier with his own thoughts for company than when in the society of men and women.

Nevertheless, there were occasions on which Hepworth went into the world. On market and fair days he mixed with men, and transacted his business in a fashion that showed him to be keenly alive to his own interests. He was a scrupulously fair dealer, but was not to be over-reached or deceived. Those who knew him as farmer and business man spoke highly and admiringly of his capabilities; he was, they said, the man to make money and to keep it. But in addition to being a strict man of business, Hepworth was also a man of religion. His ancestors for three generations had been devout and fervent Methodists, and in the peculiar tenets and dogmas of that body his mother had instructed him from infancy. His earliest acquaintance with religious literature came from the writings of Wesley and his contemporary apostles. With the Jewish scriptures he was intimate to a strange degree, and their poetry, their imagination, and their mystic influence had tended to fill his mind with something of the awful and mysterious. Never in a position to doubt the accuracy of all that had been taught to him, he accepted the whole creed of historic Christianity with something like childlike confidence. To him there was nothing questionable, nothing impossible in what he believed to be the scheme of salvation. It was a vast, magnificent poem, in which justice and mercy were blended with infinite love. He had never considered it from outside, for underneath its shadow he had always dwelt. When he was still a young man, Hepworth, moved thereto by certain impulses of his own nature and persuaded by his mother and the ministers at Sicaster, began to preach in the village chapels. There were other farmers in the neighbourhood who were occupied on Sundays in the same work. These he soon out-distanced in the path of popular appreciation, though he knew nothing of the fact himself. To hear him preach to his rustic audiences was to catch some notion of the mysterious tragedy of the world. When he escaped from himself into the region of prophecy he was half-poet and half-seer. He saw behind the veil, and the people saw with him. His lonely communings amongst the woods and fields, and his solitary pilgrimages to the distant villages where he had preaching engagements to fulfil, tended to develop in him the mysticism which had been planted in his nature by his early training, and it thus came about that when he spoke to the people his utterances came as from the hill-tops and the lonely places.

At the time of Elisabeth's coming to the Home Farm, Hepworth was living his usual quiet and solitary life. He was entirely occupied with his farming, his books and his thoughts. He was in all respects a serious and sober man, taking the colour of his life from the quiet tints that surrounded him on every side, and there was no thought of change within him. Elisabeth, who at that time had much trouble of her own, thought him the loneliest man she had ever known. He ate his meals in loneliness, he went about his farm in loneliness, and he sat alone in his parlour through the long winter evenings reading his books. He rarely conversed with any of his servants, except upon matters of business. It seemed to her that he was wrapped up in himself.

Hepworth had been attracted to Elisabeth in the hiring-fair at Sicaster by the pathetic hopelessness of her face. He felt sure that she had some secret trouble, and stood in need of help. Now that she was under his roof he watched her narrowly. Within a few days of her coming there he found that she was able to accomplish all that he had engaged her to do. She was neat, orderly, and precise, and displayed the qualities of taste and management which he desired. His table was now well-ordered, and his rooms made more habitable: he felt that if occasion arose he could bring a friend or a customer to dine with him, and count upon finding things as he wished them to be. He had a certain native taste about the details of daily life which his loneliness had developed into fads and fancies that were utterly puzzling to old Mally, whose ideas were all of the rough-and-ready order. Elisabeth satisfied him in these respects: he quickly decided that he had done well in engaging her.

Though he had never paid much attention to women, Hepworth found himself studying Elisabeth with some curiosity. He quickly became aware that she was of a superior class to that from which domestic servants are usually drawn, and that there was about her a certain refinement that gave her some claim to distinction. Now that she was constantly within his view he saw that she was an engaging young woman, with a face that had even pretensions to beauty. She was always neat and tidy, and conveyed an impression of quiet resource, as she moved about her household duties. Hepworth fancied that the first week of her residence at the farm improved her personal appearance, and that some colour was beginning to come into her pale cheeks. In spite of this, however, Elisabeth's eyes and mouth were still sad, and the pathetic look which had struck him when he first caught sight of her, remained there, and was rarely chased away.

Hepworth stood by his hearth one morning, watching Elisabeth arrange his breakfast-table. She was unaware of the scrutiny he bestowed upon her, and moved about, unconscious that he followed every detail of her work.

"You do your work very well, Elisabeth," said Hepworth, after a time. "I am very pleased with you."

Elisabeth looked up and coloured slightly at this word of praise.

"I am very glad, sir," she answered.

"I don't think you have been used to that sort of work," he said, somewhat diffidently. "At least, not to do it yourself."

Elisabeth made no answer.

"I hope you are quite comfortable here," he said. "Old Mally is rather rough, I know, and perhaps you—"

Elisabeth interrupted him hastily.

"I am very comfortable, sir, indeed I am—and Mally is very kind to me," she said. "Nobody could be kinder—and I'm glad I give you satisfaction. It was very good of you to engage me as you did—I wanted some help badly enough!" she added, with a sudden burst of confidence.

"Yes?" said Hepworth. "Then I am glad, very glad, Elisabeth. And if—perhaps I could help you further?"

Elisabeth shook her head.

"No, sir, thank you. I am much obliged to you, but you can't."

"You have had trouble, Elisabeth, you told me that, I think?"

"Yes, sir. But—it's no use, sir, I can't talk about it. It was more than trouble, and sometimes—"

She seemed to be about to say more, but suddenly stopped and hurried from the room. Hepworth looked after her with curiosity, not unmixed with pity. He wished that he had not spoken to her—it was evident that whatever trouble she had was still keen and poignant. He had supposed that it referred to the death of her husband—that much she had told him—but her last words seemed to suggest something further in the nature of mystery.

CHAPTER V
THE VILLAGE CHAPEL

On the second Sunday after Elisabeth's arrival at the farm, Mally informed her that Mr. Hepworth was to preach at the chapel of the neighbouring village that afternoon, and invited her to be present.

"You didn't stir out o' t' house last Sunday," said Mally, "but you mun göa to-däay, my lass, for it'll do you good. T' maister's a varry high-larnt man, and I don't reckon to understand all 'at he says, my-sen, but I'm sure it's good, 'cos he uses sich long words. I'll get all t' work done i' good time efter dinner and göa wi' you to hear him."

Accordingly Mally and Elisabeth set out for the village chapel early in the afternoon. The old servant was attired in her Sunday best, and was proud and pleased in consequence. She drew Elisabeth's attention to its gorgeousness as she aired each garment before the kitchen fire.

"I bowt this here gown piece," said Mally, "seven year agöa at Cornchester fair, and I've kept it for best iver sin'. That theer jack-et, now—I bowt that at t' best shop i' Sicaster when t' owd mis-sis died. It hed crape trimming then, but I tuke 'em off, and Polly Jones, 'at lives at Hornforth, an's larnin' t' dressmakin' at Sicaster, she's retrimmed it wi' black braid i' what she called t' milintary fash-ion—summat 'at t' sodgers weer, I reckon. I allus did believe i' bein' smart, you knaw. Now what do you think to my bonnet?—I've nob-but hed it fower year, so it's quite in t' fashion, as t' saying goes."

Elisabeth looked at the bonnet and said it was very nice. It was large and prodigal of design and colour, and Mally drew her atten-tion to the fact that there were no less than eight sorts of flowers in it, to say nothing of a humming-bird perched at the top of an artificial spray of some tropical plant.

"It's a bit heavy, to be sewer," said Mally. "But Lord love ye, everybody knows 'at pride's painful. If ye want to be i' t' fashion you mun mak' up your mind to be a bit uncomfortable."

They then set out for the chapel along the road which Elisabeth had travelled with Hepworth as they returned from Sicaster after the statute-hiring fair. Mally carried a hymn-book in one hand and a clean pocket-handkerchief, scented with dried lavender, in the other. She informed Elisabeth that she had a paper of mint lozenges in her pocket, and that she never went to chapel without them.

"There's nowt like heyin' summat to suck at," she said. "When t' preycher's busy wi' his firstly and secondly I can bide, but when he comes to t' thirdly and lastly I mun hev' summat i' my mouth, or else I get fidgety. So if tha' wants a lozenge, lass, tha' mun nudge my elbow, and I'll gi' thi one."

The village chapel stood near the entrance to the long street of farmsteads and cottages, and upon a slight eminence, approached by a winding path, up which several persons were slowly climbing as Mally and Elisabeth drew near. It was a quaint, four-square erection of red brick, that had been worn to a deep colour by the rain and storm of nearly a century. Above its narrow doorway a tablet of sandstone had been cemented to the wall, apparently in readiness for an inscription which was never placed there. Before the door a tiny yard or enclosure, thickly carpeted with long grass, made an open-air vestibule to the chapel. Two or three ancient men, clad in antiquated garments of sombre hue, stood about the grass, and greeted the old servant with brotherly affection. They enquired if Mr. Hepworth was coming behind.

"He'll nooän be so long," said Mally. "I'll warrant him. Ye niver fun' him late, I know. He doesn't waste nöa time, doesn't t' maister, neyther at t' fore-end nor at t' back-end. There's some 'at comes sweeätin' an' fussin' at t' last minute, and there's some 'at's theer haäf-an-hour afore t' time, and he doesn't belong to eyther o' that lot. There's some on ye hings round this chapel-door for an hour afore t' meetin', same as if ye'd nowt to do. Why don't ye go inside and read t' hymns ovver?"

With this admonition Mally passed into the chapel, followed by Elisabeth, who had never had such an experience before, and who was consequently interested in all that she heard and saw. She looked round her with curious eyes after they had taken their seats. She found herself in a square box, painted in a dull drab colour, and furnished with a hard, uncushioned seat, on which it was impossible to do otherwise than sit erect. Behind her rose four more lines of similar enclosures, with a gangway in the middle; before her lay the floor of the chapel, furnished with long, unbacked benches. Facing benches and pews stood the pulpit, a square box, approached by a short flight of stairs, and furnished with a scarlet cushion on which reposed a large Bible and a hymn-book. Everything was sombre and plain in outline and tint; the candlesticks, socketed into the tops of the pews, were of unvarnished iron, and the candles were ordinary tallow.

The chapel was already half-filled with people, and Elisabeth regarded them with some curiosity. In the pews sat two or three men of the farmer class, in broadcloth and clean linen, with their wives

34

and families ranged in order of precedence. Two or three old folks sat on the bench by the fire with their backs against the wall, a dozen children sat here and there on the unbacked benches; a group of shock-headed ploughboys occupied the seats under the pulpit. A little woman in a poke-bonnet and large spectacles sat amongst the children and kept them in order; her sharp eyes were now fixed through her spectacles upon her hymn-book and now over them at some delinquent who showed a disposition to misbehave. In the pews and on the benches there was a peculiar silence that seemed oppressive. Now and then somebody sighed—the long sigh of abstracted meditation. It seemed to Elisabeth that everybody had retired from the world to give themselves up in this quiet little place to reflection and dreamy thought.

Presently the old men who had been waiting his arrival at the door came in with Hepworth, followed by a number of people who had lingered outside until the hour of service was at hand. Hepworth took off his overcoat and ascended the pulpit-stairs. He gave out two lines of a hymn, and there was a rustling of hymn-books amongst the occupants of the pews. Amongst the people sitting on the benches rose an old man, one of those who had waited Hepworth's arrival at the door. He struck a tune in a high, quavering voice, and kept time to it with his hymn-book, and with swayings and contortions of his long, lean figure, that would have seemed ludicrous under other circumstances. All the folks joined in the singing, without regard to time or tune. Some of them got a bar or two in front, some lagged behind, but the old man persevered, rolling his eyes and waving his book until the final amen brought the performance to a close.

Elisabeth paid little attention to the devotional services which followed. The praying and the reading were constantly interrupted by ejaculations of praise and thanksgiving from the congregation; the hymns were sung after the fashion of the first. At last they were over, and Hepworth opened his Bible and gave out his text. Elisabeth forgot the high-backed, uncomfortable seat; she fixed her eyes on his face and wondered what he was going to say.

All that week Hepworth's mind had been fixed on one subject—the sure and inevitable detection of secret sin. There had come to his knowledge a case in which a man had committed grievous wrong against a fellow-being, whereby suffering had come to many people while the wrong-doer went free and unsuspected. Years had passed, and at length, when the wicked man thought himself safe, the bolt had fallen, and God's finger had pointed him out to the world with remorseless and clear indication of his guilt. That, said Hepworth, was justice. It was inevitable, nothing could prevent it. Men might sin, they might break law and commandment, and flatter themselves that no eye saw them and that no power could confound them, but their assurance was bound to come to naught. Sin meant death, righteousness meant life. In that there was comfort for those who had been wronged, and there was also warning for the evil-doer.

Hepworth's eyes, watching the faces of his congregation, suddenly caught sight of Elisabeth. She was leaning forward, her face betraying rapt attention, her eyes ablaze with new interest, her cheeks aglow with excitement. Hepworth paused, something in her eyes, meeting his for the moment, struck a new train of thought. He turned away from the denunciations which he had been uttering against the wicked, and began to plead for forgiveness for them, from those whom their wickedness had brought to sorrow or shame. It was, he said, the nature of man to sin, but it was his highest quality to forgive. He watched Elisabeth's face as he said this, it grew hard and cold, the light died away from it, the mouth became firm and rigid; it was evident that she was no longer interested or excited. But chancing to catch sight of her again as he wound up his exhortation by insisting on the sureness and certainty of punishment for the wicked, he saw that the eager look had returned, and that the interest was keen as before. He left the pulpit mystified. It seemed to him that for once at any rate he had preached to a soul which responded to more than half his thought.

Hepworth was to preach again at the evening service, and he remained in the village during the interval. Elisabeth and Mally returned home together, Mally full of quaint remarks as to her master's learning and the bad behaviour of the children on the benches, Elisabeth silent and thoughtful.

When Hepworth came home later in the evening he found Elisabeth laying his supper-table in the parlour. He sat down and watched her, and thought that he still perceived some signs in her face of the eagerness she had shown during the sermon in the afternoon. Presently the table preparations were completed, but Elisabeth lingered. She looked doubtfully at her master.

"I should like to ask you something, sir," she said diffidently. "It's been on my mind ever since this afternoon."

"What is it?" asked Hepworth.

"Do you believe all that you said this afternoon," she asked, regarding him with curiosity plainly shown in her eyes and face. "All of it?"

Hepworth looked at her and wondered.

"Yes, of course I do, Elisabeth," he answered. "All of it, every word."

"You are sure that all will be made plain in the end, some day, sooner or later?"

"Yes, I am sure."

Elisabeth shook her head.

"Don't you believe it?" he asked presently.

"No!" she said. "No, sir, I wish I could. I wish I could believe that those who work wickedness will be punished for it, as you say they will."

"They will," he answered. "It's sure and certain. It's a consequence—you can't have sin without punishment nor good without reward. Don't doubt it. But"—here he paused and remembered her changed expression of the afternoon—"we must forgive those who do wickedness against us."

The hard expression came into Elisabeth's face again. She shook her head decidedly.

"Good people may do that, sir," she said. "But if you had been tried—if you had seen wickedness, and felt yourself powerless to prevent it—if you saw the devil's hand in a thing, and God did nothing to stop him—what then?"

Before Hepworth could answer this question, Elisabeth picked up her tray and left the room. It seemed as though she had not so much wished for an answer as that he should reconsider his own position.

Hepworth pushed open the door and looked in.

CHAPTER VI
PARTIAL CONFIDENCES

Hepworth sat thinking matters over for some time without coming to any definite conclusion. There was some mystery in Elisabeth's life, he finally decided, that had made more than an ordinary impression upon her, but as he was wholly in the dark respecting it he felt unable to talk to her on the subject. He wondered what her secret was, and whether she would eventually reveal it to him. Of one thing he felt assured—the mystery that she concealed had to a certain extent embittered her existence. He had watched her closely and had been struck by the prevailing sadness of her face, which ought to have expressed nothing but happiness and light-hearted feeling. She was young and should have had few cares, Hepworth thought. He knew little of sorrow himself, and was therefore not altogether fitted to judge of it in others, but he was persuaded that Elisabeth's trouble was of an exceptional nature and was exercising a great influence upon her.

During the afternoon of the next day Hepworth was passing through the upper fold when he heard the sound of a woman's voice singing in one of the buildings. He stopped and listened wonderingly. The voice was clear and high—the tune a merry one. Everything about the farmstead at that moment was quiet and hushed—the day had reached that mystic point where the afternoon begins to melt towards evening. The men were working in the Ten-Acre; there was nobody about the place but Mally and Elisabeth and himself; therefore it must be from Elisabeth that the song came. He walked across the fold in the direction of the barn and pushed open the door and looked in. After the first glance he remained standing at the open door in some surprise and astonishment.

The barn had two doors, that at which Hepworth stood, opening from the fold, and one, exactly opposite, which gave access to the orchard. Between these doors the floor-space was covered with boards that in former days had been used as a threshing-floor. In the centre of this stood Elisabeth. She was dressed for the afternoon in a neat black dress, relieved from any suspicion of sombreness by a white muslin apron and cap. In one hand she held a measure full of grain, and she threw handfuls of this to the fowls which had followed her into the barn and now grouped themselves, feeding and clucking, at her feet. Now and then she threw a handful with wider sweep to the pigeons who strutted at the entrance to the orchard, or to the sparrows that had flown down from the bare-branched apple-trees and came timidly towards the barn-door. As she thus occupied herself she sang, but after he had caught sight of her Hepworth was not so much interested in her singing as in her face. For the first time since he had seen it the expression of grief and sorrow was gone and in its place there was life and animation. Elisabeth's cheeks were full of colour; her eyes danced with pleasure, smiles curved her lips as she flung the grain amongst the birds at her feet: Hepworth suddenly recognised that she was a pretty and even fascinating woman. He pushed open the door and advanced into the barn: Elisabeth turned and caught sight of him. She stopped singing, and at the same moment the pigeons and sparrows, frightened by Hepworth's entrance, flew away above the trees outside. The fowls stayed there and pecked at the stray grains with undisturbed industry. Elisabeth gave a little laugh and flung the grain which remained in the measure amongst them in a heap.

"You are busy, Elisabeth," said Hepworth.

He stood close by and looked at her curiously. There was something new in her whole appearance, even in the way in which her colour slightly increased as she turned to him.

"I am only feeding the fowls, sir," she answered.

"And singing," he said.

"There's no work in that, sir," she replied.

"No, but I never heard you sing before—as you were going about the house, I mean," he said, scarcely knowing what was in his mind.

"I haven't sung for a long time," she said.

"Then I suppose you sing to-day because you feel light-hearted," said Hepworth. "Your song was a merry one, at any rate."

Elisabeth laughed. There was something in the sound that seemed to jar on Hepworth's mind; he looked more attentively at her, and found that over her face had come something of the hard expression with which he was already familiar.

"I don't know about light-hearted, sir," she said. "It's such a long time since I knew what light-heartedness meant. But I've felt glad since yesterday—and I'm hopeful of something—and so I suppose I began singing."

"What made you glad?" he asked, leaning against the door of the barn and watching her more intently.

Elisabeth gave him a quick look.

"What you said at the chapel, sir," she replied. "I thought about it, and I think you're right, and so I was pleased, because I wanted to think it before, only I never could bring my mind to it."

"Oh," said Hepworth. "And what was it that I said—about forgiving those who sin against us?"

Elisabeth shook her head with a decided activity.

"No, sir, no! It's no use preaching that to *me*—saints might do it, but I can't. No—it was what you said about those who do wrong in secret, thinking that they will never be found out and that they will escape punishment. You said that punishment would come to them. I wanted to believe that a long time, but I never could, and I shouldn't now, only you seemed so certain about it."

"Elisabeth," said Hepworth, "why didn't you believe it? Your ideas are new to me—I never met with them."

Elisabeth looked at him with an air of doubtfulness.

"Perhaps, sir," she answered, with evident simplicity, "you don't know much of the world?"

"I am a man of middle age," he said.

She shook her head and smiled.

"I don't think *that's* got much to do with it, sir. It all depends, doesn't it, on how much a person's seen of life?"

"Have you seen so much that you know these things better than I do?" he enquired.

"Oh no, sir; I don't say that. I only say that from what I've seen during my life I've never been able to see that all you preached yesterday is true."

Hepworth reflected. He was always curiously interested in these matters, and had an almost morbid curiosity in any question affecting the relation of the human soul to belief.

"You mean," he said, "that you can't reconcile your own experiences of life with the teachings of religion?"

"Yes, sir, I suppose that is how you would put it."

"But why, Elisabeth?"

"Oh, for many reasons, sir. Now you say that God is good, and that He's the Father of all, don't you?"

Hepworth nodded his head.

"I suppose you believe that," said Elisabeth, "and so did I, once, because I was never taught anything else. But afterwards I didn't, because I couldn't. If God was Father of everybody, couldn't He protect those that never did anyone any harm? Wouldn't He act like a father?"

"Yes."

"Then why doesn't He?" she asked with sudden fierceness. "Why, why? Why do wicked people flourish and go free, and become

41

prosperous, and those who are innocent suffer for their wickedness? Why, sir?"

Hepworth shook his head. He was neither prepared nor able to answer such a question.

"That's why I couldn't believe those things," said Elisabeth. "I heard them preached and talked about, but it wasn't so in real life."

"We don't know all that God knows," said Hepworth. "It may be that what we call evil is working for good."

Elisabeth made an involuntary gesture of impatient dissent.

"I'm not clever enough to see that, sir," she said. "But if you'd known what I've known, you'd know how I feel about it. Supposing you saw an innocent man suffer for a guilty one, and knew what pain and anguish he must suffer, and had to suffer yourself because of it, and prayed to God, oh, night and day, to make things right, and there was no answer, no answer, nothing but silence and helplessness—what then, sir?"

Hepworth stared at her in amazement. She spoke with vehemence, her bosom rose and fell as if under the influence of strong emotion, her mouth quivered pathetically as she spoke of suffering and helplessness.

"Elisabeth?" he exclaimed, forgetting his usual reserve. "You've been through all that yourself! What was it?"

But Elisabeth suddenly regained her composure. She had laid down the grain-measure on a sack of corn close by, while she spoke—she now picked it up and made for the barn-door.

"I beg your pardon, sir," she said, her tone implying the recognition of the position which she occupied in Hepworth's household. "I've been forgetting myself, I'm afraid, and talking too much. But you spoke kindly, and—and I've no friend to talk to now."

"You can look on me as a friend," said Hepworth. "And if you are in trouble—"

"I've no trouble now, sir, that can be shared or mended. It's only the memory of one, and I shall tell it to nobody," she said, with decision. "I've taken it to heart badly so far, but I'm feeling better since I heard what you said yesterday. I've thought that over, and I believe one thing—*the wicked shall be found out*."

She uttered these words with such an expression of fervent hope, not unmixed with something like hate, that Hepworth could only remain silent and wondering. She went out of the barn, and in another moment he heard her singing as she crossed the fold.

Hepworth sat up late that night reading in his parlour, and when he went to bed the house was silent and dark. As he gained the head of the staircase and turned into the long passage that ran the length of the house, he was attracted by a gleam of light that came from a door-way. He walked down the passage towards it, thinking that someone had forgotten to turn out a lamp. He came to the open door and suddenly found that he was looking into Elisabeth's room.

The door stood slightly ajar: Elisabeth had forgotten to secure it before retiring. By arrangement with old Mally she burned a lamp through the night. The lamp stood on a bracket just within the door, its light faint and low, but sufficiently clear to give Hepworth a partial view of the room. Without knowing it he had looked in and his eyes fell upon Elisabeth asleep, with the faint light full upon her face.

Hepworth stood still for a moment. She was sleeping quietly, her dark hair strewn about the pillow, her bosom rising and falling in regular movements, one arm thrown upward above her head. Whatever her trouble, she had lost it in sleep.

He stood and looked, and as he looked a sudden consciousness came over him. There was a new interest within him; he loved this woman whom he had met so strangely. For some days he had felt an unknown influence coming into his life; now at the sight of that innocent sleep, it suddenly burnt up within him into strong flame, and for the first time in his life Hepworth recognised the influence of passionate desire to love and to be loved. He looked and looked again, and suddenly closed the door with a gentle movement and went to his own room, full of new thoughts.

PART THE SECOND

WHERE HIGHWAYS MEET

CHAPTER I
ST. THOMAS'S DAY

To a man of Hepworth's peculiar temperament the discovery which he had just made was full of the most remarkable meaning. For many days he went about his business, or sat in his lonely room thinking it over. In all his thought there was never any doubt as to his exact feeling for Elisabeth. That he loved her he felt certain; that he should continue to love her, and only her, he felt equally sure. That which he had never expected to encounter, and for which he had formerly felt no desire, had now come to him, and filled up all his life.

Being accustomed from childhood to self-examination, and to a certain introspection which he sometimes carried to the verge of morbid feeling, Hepworth at this period subjected his own emotions to a strict dissection. He found himself at forty years of age in love with a young woman who was a perfect stranger to him as regarded her history and antecedents. He wondered why he should fall in love with her. Was it some turn of her head, some note in her voice, some trick of the eye? If so, why did any of these things appeal to him? He had seen prettier women, not once, but a score of times—fresher, sweeter, more attractive. Why, if this one attracted him, did not they? He could say honestly that he had never been attracted by any woman's physical beauty: if he had noticed it, it had been as other men notice pictures—with a passing glance that stopped at admiration. But now there was a different feeling within him. He analysed that feeling mercilessly, concealing nothing of it from his speculative mind.

"Here I am," said he, as he walked the fields, or sat alone through the long evening, "a man of nigh on middle age, content until recently to live as lonely a life as ever a hermit could desire. I knew nothing of women—certainly I never wanted one. In the matter of love they were unknown to me. I never supposed that I should care to think of one in that way. And now here is this woman, whose sorrowful face attracted me to her at first, filling me with a new attraction. She is not a girl, I know she has been married already, and that she may have no more love to give, and yet I have a feeling for her that I never had for anything in my life. That feeling is a feeling of want. I want Her—not some other woman, but Her. I want all of Her—body, soul, mind. And now I know something that I never dreamed of till she came—I shall not be myself, my life will not be full and complete, unless she and I come together in one life."

Hepworth continued this analysis of his own thoughts and feelings for many days, but he never arrived at any other conclusion than that which made itself evident at first. There was now a want in his life which only Elisabeth could satisfy. As he had already recognised, it was not some other woman, not woman in the abstract, but her. He made no attempt to explain this mystery to himself, but accepted it and waited.

For some weeks he said nothing to Elisabeth of the thoughts which filled his mind. They maintained their relations as master and servant, she with perfect sincerity, knowing nothing of the feeling which she had inspired, he with a sort of curious delight in being waited upon by the woman he loved. Hepworth indeed found a strange pleasure in the secrecy of his new feelings and emotions. He rarely conversed with Elisabeth save on the most ordinary topics, but he watched her occasionally as she went about her duties. The quiet and regular life of the lonely farmstead had exerted an improving influence upon her—she was by that time a well-favoured, even pretty woman, likely to catch the eye of any man with an eye for beauty. Hepworth noticed this, but paid little heed to it. He was not insensible to physical beauty, and indeed appreciated it keenly as all men who suddenly emerge from loneliness and self-inspection must, but his feeling was deeper, and could not be explained by the fact that Elisabeth had regained her pretty looks and bright eyes.

It is the fashion in these parts for the old women of the parish to band themselves together upon the morning of St. Thomas's Day, and to go from farm to farm gathering contributions towards a general fund which is subsequently divided amongst them in equal shares. Hepworth's farmstead being situated some distance from the nearest village, a deputation from the band came to him, walking through the snow in the early morning in order to collect his contribution. Elisabeth summoned him from the parlour when the old women arrived, and Hepworth left his breakfast to attend to them. They were three in number, and they sat on chairs before the kitchen fire warming hands and feet, and complaining of the bitter weather. One was wrapped closely in a man's greatcoat, and had tied up her poke-bonnet about her ears with a shawl; another wore a stout piece of sacking over her shoulders; the third had encased her feet in successive layers of stout stocking, drawn over the boots, until she resembled an Esquimaux. Each rose and curtsied profoundly as Hepworth entered the kitchen.

"Now, then," said Hepworth. "Come again, eh? Why, it isn't a year since you were here, is it? The doorstep'll never cool of you at this rate."

This was a pleasantry made upon every such occasion, and each old woman laughed at it as a matter of course. Having laughed, they sighed profoundly.

"Poor folks, Mestur Hepworth, poor folks, ye know!" said one. "We mun keep t' owd customs up for wer own sakes, ye know. T' cowd's that bitter, and coals is that dear, and poverty's a sharp tooith, as the saying goes."

"I'll be bound you don't know much about that, Nanny," said Hepworth. "I expect you've got an old stocking-foot somewhere that's pretty well lined, eh?"

"Nay, not me!" said Nanny. "I never see'd a real golden pound i' my life to call my own. If I hed one somebody else allus hed a call on it."

"Stockin'-feet mak's poor purses," said the second old woman. "They tak' so much fillin'."

"Aye, and now-a-days," said the third, "there's nowt to fill 'em wi'. Times is hard for poor folk."

"Well," said Hepworth, "I suppose you've all had your breakfasts and can't eat any more, can you?"

"None o' your fun-makkin', maister," said Mally, who stood by, busily engaged in cooking preparations. "Eh, dear, men are allus i' t' way. As if there worn't some hot spiced ale all ready for 'em on t' oven top."

As the old women had already seen the hot spiced ale referred to, this was no news to them, but they, nevertheless, manifested much interest in its removal to the table by the fire, and in the spice-bread and cheese which was placed beside it. When each had laid hold of a pint-mug filled with Mally's hot brew, they offered Hepworth their best respects, and wished him a long life.

"And if I might mak' so bold," said Nanny, "and I nursed you, mestur, when you was an infant in arms, I might say 'at I hope you'll be a wed man come next Thomas's Day."

"That's an important matter, Nanny," said Hepworth. "Why do you wish it?"

"Naäy," said Nanny, "I ha' no opinion o' single men—saving your presence. I like to see a man wi' a wife and a houseful of bairns—that's summut like. Lord bless ye, that's what the good Book says. I went to t' church last Sunday, and they were reading t' Psalms—'happy is he,' they read, ' 'at hes his quiver full on 'em.' "

"Aye," sighed the second old woman, "it all depends. It wor all varry weel for David to write that, 'cause he wor a king, and hed all t' money 'at he wanted, and house-room, and all; but it's different wi'

49

poor folk. I've hed ten i' my time, and they tak' a deal o' bringing up."

"I've hed twelve," said Nanny, stoutly. "And I niver browt 'em up at all—they browt theirsens up. Bairns is like weeds—leave 'em alone, and they'll grow apace."

Mally now remarked that she had never heard such rubbish talked in all her born days. She was busily engaged in making pork-pies, and the old women were in her way, and the kitchen was further filled up by Hepworth and Elisabeth. She wanted each of them out of the way, and further resented the old women's remarks as to the blessed-ness of the married state, for she herself had never enjoyed it. Nanny understanding this, and remembering that they looked to Mally for a pitcher of hot ale every Thomas's Day, gave the signal for departure. Hepworth followed her to the door with the money for which they had walked so far. Old Nanny clutched the hand which held it out to her.

"Mestur," quoth she, with an air of mysterious import, "you mun tak' my advice about bein' wed. You mon't mind me, an owd woman 'at nursed you. Now, there's a fine young woman there"—she nod-ded her poke-bonnet in Elisabeth's direction—"why not wed her? Tak' my advice, mestur—owd folk knows more nor young uns."

Hepworth went back to his parlour and watched the three old women plodding through the snow that lay thick in the paddock. He was half inclined to be angry that people should so constantly give him advice as to his future; but Nanny's counsel, sly and good-hu-moured, seemed to fit with his present mood. He stood watching Elisabeth as she cleared his table. Life with her, he thought, would suit all his tastes and inclinations. Why not tell her of all that was in his heart?

"What did you think of the old women, Elisabeth?" he asked. Elisabeth looked up from the table and smiled.

"I thought them very amusing, sir," she answered.

"It is a custom they have hereabouts," he said. "They come every St. Thomas's Day. You never heard it spoken of, perhaps?"

"No, sir."

"That shows you are not a countrywoman," he said, smiling at her.

"No, sir, I am not—I never saw much of the country until I came here."

"Well, how do you like the country now that you do see it? Is it lonely and quiet?"

"I think it is both quiet and lonely, sir. But then—"

"Well?"

"Some people like to be quiet and lonely—I am one of them."

"Ah!" he said, with a certain feeling of satisfaction. "You don't mind the loneliness—you wouldn't object to live here—all your life, eh, Elisabeth?"

Elisabeth glanced at him curiously. From his gaze she turned to the window and looked out at the great black beech-trees rising from the white carpet of snow to the grey, monotonous sky above. There was a strange look in her eyes as she looked at him again.

"Once," she said, with a faint emphasis on the word, "once I should have objected to such a life. The loneliness of it would have killed me. But now—"

"Well, Elisabeth?"

"Now I should not mind it—I could live here always."

Something in her expression prompted him to ask her why this difference in her feelings had come.

"Why should you think differently?" he said.

"Because all places are alike—to me," she answered.

Hepworth said no more. It was plain to him, ill-versed in woman's ways as he was, that this woman had no thought of him.

"Eh, bless thy bonny face," said the old shepherd.

CHAPTER II
HEPWORTH SPEAKS

It was Hepworth's custom to give a supper to all his farm-hands with their wives and families at Christmas, and during the next few days Mally and Elisabeth were busily engaged in making the necessary preparations. Mally at that time spoke but rarely: her mind was entirely given up to the making of pies, the roasting of great joints of beef that were to go cold in the larder, and the dressing of geese and turkeys intended for the spit. She hurried here and there, always busy and preoccupied, and for four days her temper was short and her speech abrupt.

"When folks is busy," said she, deeming some explanation due to Elisabeth, "they'd owt t' be let alone. Nowt moythers me worse than hevin' to think and talk. One thing at a time—that's what I say—but it's what I can't get. There's t' pork-pies, an t' mince-pies, and t' renderin', and there's seein' after Tom when he comes to salt t' pig down, and I'm fair capped which way to turn. But t' plum-puddin's is made, and thank the Lord for that!"

Hepworth believed in keeping Christmas after the whole-hearted fashion of his ancestors, and in pursuance of his faith he caused parlour and kitchens to be lavishly decorated with green-stuff. Elisabeth found congenial employment in this: with the mysteries of the kitchen she was by no means familiar, but in anything that required taste or nicety her capabilities showed themselves to be fully adequate. Hepworth coming in on Christmas eve from Sicaster market found his parlour decorated in new fashion.

"I see you have been busy, Elisabeth," he remarked when she came in with his tea-tray. "Usually our decorations have been of the rough-and-ready description. A bough of holly stuck here, and a sprig of yew stuck there, is all that either Mally or I have dared to attempt. Now I shall expect you to decorate the kitchen for the Christmas supper. I am minded to have great doings that night, Elisabeth, and I want everything to look well."

As a result of these instructions Elisabeth persuaded Mally to hand over the great kitchen to her care, early on the afternoon of the feast. She swept and dusted it herself, and decorated the bare walls with as much care as she had bestowed on the walls of the parlour. This done she sought the aid of one of the men-servants in setting-up the tables, of which there were two, with a crosstable for the master.

She had some difficulty with Mally as to the covering of these tables. Mally was of opinion that a coarse cloth was good enough for the men and their wives: Elisabeth urged that Mr. Hepworth would expect to see everything as it ought to be. Eventually Mally gave way, on the express understanding that Elisabeth was to be responsible for the washing and ironing of the table-linen used.

"And a nice job it'll be, after that crew's eaten off 'em!" said Mally. "I know 'em—they'll set their mugs and pint-pots on t' table-cloth and mak' rings o' stale beer all over it, and they'll spill t' gravy on it an' all. Howsumiver, tha mun hev thy way, lass, and I expect t' maister'll back thee up."

She said this with a sly look at Elisabeth, for Mally was a keen observer and had noticed Hepworth's interest in the young woman. Elisabeth, however, was all unconscious of Mally's meaning: she departed to busy herself with the final preparations for the feast.

At six o'clock when all the folk had assembled and taken their places, with Hepworth at their head, the old kitchen assumed quite a gay and animated appearance. Every man, woman, and child wore his or her best: every face reflected much application of soap-and-water; every mouth widened to an anticipatory smile. Hepworth carved at one end of the table, and his foreman at the other; Mally and Elisabeth acted as waiters. It had been their particular desire to do so: Hepworth would have wished them to sit down with the rest, but Mally declared that she had no stomach after so much cooking, and Elisabeth had asked to be allowed to share Mally's duties. Each took a table, and each was kept continually going.

Elisabeth looked very attractive that night, the animation of the scene, the continual chatter, and the unrestrained laughter of the lads and lasses, had brought fresh colour to her cheeks, and new light to her eyes. In the white apron that covered her neat black dress she had stuck a sprig of scarlet-berried holly: this gave her an air of smartness that was fascinating.

"Eh, bless thy bonny face!" said the old shepherd, as she helped him to a second plate of turkey. "I could wish I wor young ageëan!"

Hepworth caught the remark, and glanced at Elisabeth, who was smiling at the old man's compliment. It struck a new chord in his nature to hear her admired, and he suddenly recognised that he was proud of her good looks, and was pleased that other men paid homage to them.

"Owd Tommy's gotten a soft spot in his heart," said one of the lads, nudging his fellow at the table.

Old Tommy heard and shook his grey head.

"Aye," said he, pipingly. "Aye, there's some on us owd uns 'at can see bewty a deëal quicker nor some o' ye young uns. When I wor nobbut a lad I hed a sweetheart, but now-a-days t' lads is shyer nor t' lasses—sure-ly. Ye nooän on ye come forrard, ye young uns, so us owd uns has to dew it for ye. I nobbut wish I wor younger—I'd show ye how to mak' love to t' lasses."

The women laughed at old Tommy's pleasantries, and Hepworth, anxious to make all at their ease, laughed with them. But he began to wonder, while he laughed, if a man of his sober years had any right to talk of love to a young woman. It came upon him with sudden directness that he was no longer young himself, and that Elisabeth, whom he loved, was little more than a girl.

Hepworth's humble guests had all gone by ten o'clock, and he stood alone in his parlour thinking over the events of the evening. One of the labourers' wives in a fit of mischief had tied a sprig of mistletoe to the great rafter that ran across the kitchen, and the lads and lasses had made the most of it. Once Elisabeth had allowed herself to be caught by one of the lads, amidst universal laughter. Hepworth himself had smiled at the lad's sheepish face and at the demure way in which Elisabeth held up her cheek to be kissed. He caught himself wondering what she would say if he kissed her, and turned hot and red at the thought of it. In all his life the only woman's lips that had ever touched his own were the lips of his mother. While he stood by the fire thinking in this unusual way, Elisabeth came in. Mally, she said, was tired out and had gone to bed, and she had come to ask if there was anything that he wanted.

"Nothing," he answered. "Nothing—thank you. But—stay a moment, Elisabeth; I want to speak to you."

She stood waiting, in evident expectation of some order or instruction. Hepworth felt nervously uncertain of himself; the intensity of his feeling seemed to destroy his hold over his own faculties.

"Shut the door, Elisabeth," he said, "and come in—there's something I wished to tell you to-night."

She obeyed his instructions and came a little nearer, leaning one hand on the table between them and looking at him for his orders. Hepworth made an effort to speak.

"Elisabeth," he said, "you said the other day—when the old women had been a-Thomasing, wasn't it?—that you would be content to stay here. You said that, Elisabeth, didn't you?"

He made such an effort to speak calmly that as yet she did not notice his agitation.

"Yes, sir," she answered.

"And do you still feel like that?" he asked.

"Yes, sir," she said again.

"Then stay," he said, his voice falling almost to a whisper. "Stay, Elisabeth, stay always—be my wife!"

He stepped towards her as he spoke and held out his hands to her across the table. Elisabeth started and drew back, but he saw that it was only in surprise. He came up to the table and leaned on it for support. The lamp stood between him and Elisabeth and threw a strong light on their faces, his full of intense and eager passion that left his cheeks colourless and his lips trembling, hers suddenly stricken with a surprise that seemed to be mingled with painful thought.

"Stop," he said, "don't speak, Elisabeth. Let me say all that I meant to say. Stay with me, Elisabeth: be my wife, for I love you. See, I know nothing about love, I don't even know how to tell you these things—they're strange to me. What I've just said to you I never said before to any woman. But—you I want; you, and nobody and nothing else. Oh, you don't know, perhaps, what it is to feel like that! See, Elisabeth, of late I've thought of nothing but you: you seem to fill my mind so that nothing else can come there. And somehow—perhaps it's because I have never known anything of love before, I seem to feel that, if you are beyond me, I shall never be satisfied—never! Oh, my dear, just think what it is to feel like that—and I a man that's gone all these years and never so much as turned his head to look at a woman. Elisabeth—I never thought to feel these things—they're a mystery to me. But I do feel them, perhaps all the keener because they've been slow to come—and now I want you to love and keep."

He had spoken hurriedly and in a low voice, and now he paused for breath. Elisabeth, who had watched and listened in undisguised amazement, was about to speak. He lifted his hand, motioning her to stop.

"Wait," he said, as if conscious that he dreaded to hear what she might say. "Wait, Elisabeth. There are other things that I would like to say. Elisabeth, you'll believe that all I say is honest and true? I suppose it must have been from the first that I loved you—from that day at Sicaster. I looked and saw you, and you were unhappy—forgive me for speaking of it—and my heart seemed to go out to you, Elisabeth. And then bit by bit it came, and at last I knew it very suddenly. Elisabeth, when a man loves at my age, he loves once for all. It's not a whim nor a fancy—and oh, it's hard to conquer! Elisabeth—"

He said no more, but held out his hands across the table. Elisabeth looked at him, strangely moved, but she made no sign of giving him her hands.

"Mr. Hepworth," she said gently, "it's no good, sir, speaking to me like that."

"Ah!" he said.

"Don't mistake me, sir," she said quickly. "I believe all you've said, and—and any woman would have been proud to hear it said to her. You are a man to love—I'll say that frankly—and the woman who takes you will get a good man. But you must not ask me, sir."

"Why—why, Elisabeth," he said.

"Consider, Mr. Hepworth," she answered. "Why, you don't even know me! I'm your parlour-maid—"

"Oh!" he exclaimed. "Let us hear no more of that, Elisabeth. If that is all—"

"It's not all," she said, gravely.

"Tell me," he said, "is there anything between us?"

She did not answer him for a moment, but stood regarding him steadily. Then—

"Yes," she said. "There is. I am married already, and I do not know whether my dear husband is dead or living."

CHAPTER III
ELISABETH'S HISTORY

When Elisabeth uttered these words, Hepworth knew that his doom was spoken. He turned away and sank down in his chair, and dropped his face in his hands. Elisabeth stood in the same attitude, watching him attentively. For some moments neither spoke.

"Mr. Hepworth," said Elisabeth at last, "I'm sorry that you should have come to think of me in the way you have, and yet I'm glad in one way, because it gives me the chance of telling you about myself—and that'll be a relief to me, God knows. I've thought a good deal about that lately. Sometimes I've thought I was doing wrong in living here under false colours—it seemed to me that I ought to tell you all my story. I've meant to do it, many a time, but one thing or another stopped me. At first when I found what a comfortable home I'd got here I was afraid to speak, because—well, I won't say why, now, because I was quite wrong. Afterwards I was on the point of speaking more than once, and then it seemed that it might be presumption on my part to trouble you with my affairs. But now that you have said what you have, I think I should like to tell you my story—that is, if you'll listen to it."

Hepworth raised his head and looked at her. His face was wan and haggard in the lamp-light; it seemed to her that he had suddenly aged.

"Tell me, Elisabeth," he said. "Tell me whatever you choose. I am your friend, remember, and if I can do anything to help you I will."

"I am sure of that," she said, "but there's nobody that can help me—now. The sorrow that I've had! I'm past crying over it now, but once I used to lie awake the whole night long and just cry and cry until I was too tired even to do that. Then I got hard and careless, and I hated everything—just as I hate somebody now."

"Yes," said Hepworth. "I remember that I thought as much when we talked that day in the barn. I wondered at it then, because—"

"You won't wonder, sir, when you hear what I have to tell you," she said, quickly.

"Sit down and tell me about it," he said. "I should like to know."

She hesitated for a moment, and then took a chair near the table. There was a book lying close to her hand that Hepworth had left there some hours before, and as she spoke she took it up and turned the leaves over aimlessly. Something in the action suggested to him the hopelessness of the tale that she told.

"It's hard to begin what I have to tell," she said, "but it will be harder to go on with it, because it brings back things that I've tried to forget. I told you, Mr. Hepworth, that my name was Elisabeth Verrell. That was true—my husband was Walter Verrell. When I first knew him he was a clerk in one of the Bristol banks, and I was learning the dressmaking business in Bristol. I don't remember now how it was that we first met, but I have no relations of my own living, and I had had a lonely life as a girl, and when I got to know Walter it was nice to have a friend. We used to spend our spare time and our holidays together, and at last he asked me to be his wife, and I said yes without a minute's hesitation, because I loved him."

She paused for a moment, and Hepworth saw that tears had come into her eyes. He turned his head away. In his own heart there was a strange feeling. To hear her speak in this way of another man seemed to arouse a sense of jealousy within him. He had allowed himself to regard her as his own, and the sudden shock which came to him when she spoke of her husband created new impressions in his mind.

Elisabeth resumed.

"You will understand," she said, "that we were poor when we married, Walter and I. His salary was a hundred pounds a year. I wanted to go on working at my business, for a while at any rate, but he wouldn't hear of it. We had nice rooms, and we furnished them ourselves, and we were very happy in them. We were all to ourselves then, and we never wanted anybody else, because—"

"Yes," said Hepworth. "I think I know what you mean. Go on."

"Well, sir," continued Elisabeth, looking at him wonderingly, as if she did not quite understand his interruption, "everything went well with us for a while. I think things began to go wrong as soon as Stephen Wood came to see us. He was a clerk in Water's bank, and Walter looked upon him as his closest friend. One night he brought him home to supper, and after that he came constantly. You wouldn't have thought, to look at that man, Mr. Hepworth, that he was bad. He had a nice, smooth way of talking, and he was always good company, and Walter was fond of him. When I used to think all these things over afterwards, that was the thing I couldn't understand—that Walter should have been fond of this man. For Walter himself was as simple-hearted as a child, while Stephen Wood was—well, may God reward him for what he was!"

She said these words with such vehemence that Hepworth turned and gazed at her in astonishment. Her face was just then full of vindictive hate; her eyes assumed the fierce, eager expression that he had seen in them in the village chapel. She paused a moment, and seemed to recall her thoughts to other matters.

"Well, sir," she continued, "we had been married nearly a year, and I was expecting my child to be born, when a man came one morning to tell me that my husband had been arrested on a charge of forgery. I never understood all the ins and outs of the matter, but I think they said that Walter had signed the firm's name to a bill, and had collected the money and used it himself. Of course it was a lie from beginning to end, but the man who paid the money had been brought to the bank to identify the man he paid it to, and he picked out Walter at once, and nothing could shake him—he was certain of it. I believe he really did think he was right, but he was wrong for all that."

Elisabeth paused again, apparently sorely moved by these recollections, and it was some minutes before she proceeded.

"Well, sir, they took Walter before the magistrates, and he had a solicitor to defend him, but he did nothing. You see, they wanted to know where Walter was at the time the money was collected, which was at noon, when he left the bank for an hour. Now, I was not well that day, and he had been anxious about me, and had run home to see how I was. If only someone had seen him that could have sworn to him it would have saved him! But no one did see him but myself, and of course they said my evidence was nothing. So they committed him to the Assizes—"

Elisabeth began to weep at this point. Hepworth sat and watched her, with a wild longing to take her in his arms and bid her sob out her sorrow on his breast. The sight of her tears moved him strangely. Twice he tried to speak, but could find no words. So they sat there, silent, until Elisabeth recovered her composure, and went on.

"I was taken ill at that time," she said, "and my child was born—dead—and for some time they thought I was going to die too. But I got better, and then I asked for news of my husband. Mr. Hepworth, the Assizes were over, and they had tried him, and found him guilty, and the judge had sentenced him to five years' penal servitude."

Hepworth thought she would break down again at this point. But she went on hurriedly, as though she feared to linger over details.

"I didn't cry after that, sir, though I had wept day and night before. I grew hard and angry, for it seemed to me that we were friendless. And I gave up believing in God, because I felt certain that if there was a God he would never allow innocent people to go through such misery as we were enduring."

When she said this Elisabeth looked up at Hepworth with something of defiance in her eyes. She was clearly remembering the discussion she had had with him after his sermon in the village chapel. Hepworth remembered it too, but in face of her trouble and the story she had told he could say nothing.

"Well, sir," she continued, "things went on for a while until I was better, and then I had to sell up our home to pay the lawyers who defended my husband, and I had to begin earning my own living. It was then that Stephen Wood began coming to see me again. I had heard that he used to call and enquire after me when I was ill, and so I wasn't sorry to see him again, for he seemed to be the only friend we had. After I found work at my own business he used to meet me sometimes and walk to my lodgings with me. I didn't know what he was then. But I soon found out, for one night he came to my rooms on some pretence or other, and he told me that he loved me and asked me to go away with him to America. I was so amazed at his wickedness that I couldn't answer him at first, and he went on to say that it was folly for me to waste five years on Walter, who might never come out of prison again—yes, he said that!—and that if I would only go away with him, he would take me where no one could find us. Then I ordered him to leave the house that instant, and he laughed at me. I knew him, then, sir, for what he was. I could have forgiven him a good deal, because if a man loves a woman he'll say things that—well, that he wouldn't say otherwise—but I couldn't forgive him for laughing at my sorrow and trouble. I knew him then to be bad and heartless.

"Well, sir, it's no good dwelling on that matter. I got rid of him, then, but he came again, and he waylaid me in the streets, and at last, when I'd one day told him that I would never speak to him again, no matter what he did or said, he told me that I was a fool to wait for Walter, for he'd embezzled the money to give to another woman. That made me hate him—because I knew it was a lie. Thank God! I never believed it for a moment. But it suggested an idea to me. It was Stephen Wood himself that had committed the crime. He wasn't unlike Walter; they might have passed for brothers. I could see it all, and I knew why Stephen Wood had professed his friendship for the man he betrayed.

"I left Bristol, after that, sir, and come to Clothford, where one of my friends had set up a business. I was safe there from Stephen Wood, and I was comfortably provided for until my friend died. The person who took her business over, failed to carry it on, and I was in sore straits until that day you met me in Sicaster market-place. Since then you know my story.

"But now, sir, about my husband. Mr. Hepworth, I don't know, oh, I wish I did!—whether he's alive or dead. For, oh, sir, when he had been in prison nearly two years he tried to escape, and they followed him over the moors and shot at him—and—and some time after they found a body, and they said it was his—and—and—"

Here Elisabeth brought her story to an end. She suddenly burst into a storm of passionate weeping. Hepworth looked at her for a moment, and then he rose softly and left the room.

CHAPTER IV
NO OBSTACLES

Hepworth returned after a time. Elisabeth still sat by the table. She had bent her head over her folded arms and still wept, but quietly, like a child that is worn out with pain. Hepworth went up to her and laid his hand lightly on her head.

"My poor lass!" he said. "My poor lass!"

At his touch Elisabeth gave over weeping. She raised her head and began to dry her tears. But she still remained sitting at the table and showed no disposition to go away. Hepworth crossed over to the fireside and stood there watching her.

"I wish I could do something to help you," he said, presently. "God knows I would if I could."

"And I'm sure of it, sir," said Elisabeth. "But it's no good. Nothing can help me—nothing. If I could only be satisfied—if I only knew that my poor boy was dead, I think I could rest, but I don't know it, and, oh, Mr. Hepworth, the feeling is a terrible one."

"Yes," he answered. "I think I know what you feel, Elisabeth. But—"

He paused unable to say more. He had been about to tell her to have faith in God that all would come right. Half-an-hour previously he would have used the conventional words with glib ease, never doubting them, but something in the story which she had told him made him desist. He found himself in some respects sharing Elisabeth's wondering doubt. Why were these things allowed? Why was wickedness permitted to work against the peace and well-being of the innocent? Why did the wicked man flourish as a green-bay tree, while the guiltless worked out his life in tears and sorrow? The thought of it stayed him from offering the formal consolations of religion to the woman before him. To do so would have seemed the right thing to him before that night—after listening to Elisabeth's story it appeared futile, even unfitting. And so he stood there watching her and could think of nothing to say.

Elisabeth rose at last and turned to Hepworth.

"It was kind of you, sir," she said, "to listen to what I've had to tell you. I think it's done me good—it's hard to carry secrets like that about, and you're the first person to hear of mine. Perhaps—"

She paused and looked at him doubtfully.

"What is it, Elisabeth?" he asked.

"I thought, sir, that perhaps, now you know my story, you—you wouldn't care—"

"I don't know what you mean," he said, looking at her in some astonishment.

"I mean that you may not like me to stay here," she said.

"No—no!" said Hepworth. "Don't say that, Elisabeth, I shouldn't like you to think of me in that way. I want you to regard me as your friend. Would that be a friendly action? Come—come, don't talk like that."

"You're very kind, sir," she answered. "I'll serve you, Mr. Hepworth, faithfully, as long as you like to employ me."

"That will be as long as you like to stay, Elisabeth," he said.

He went across the room and held out his hand to her. She took it timidly, and looked at him with something of nervous shyness in her eyes. "Elisabeth," said Hepworth, still holding her hand, "I can't forget—what I told you to-night, you know. It's all true, that, aye, and more true now than it was when I first spoke. But, of course, it's no good now."

"No, sir," she answered in a low voice.

"I thought to be your lover," he said, "and in time your husband, Elisabeth. Oh, my dear, I love you as truly as ever a man loved a woman in this world. And now, as I can't be either husband or lover, let me be your friend, Elisabeth. Let me help you if I can. Will you?"

"Yes," she said. "I will. Why shouldn't I? There's no one else. You're all the friend I have."

"Good-night, Elisabeth," he said.

"Good-night, Mr. Hepworth," she answered.

He released her hand and she turned away. At the door she stopped and looked at him.

"I am grateful," she said, "and I wish—I wish for your sake that—that I could do what you wish."

Then she disappeared and Hepworth was alone. He sat down by the dying fire and thought. Usually he smoked a pipe of tobacco before going to bed, but that night he forgot it and sat staring listlessly at the red ashes. It seemed to him that years had gone by since he said good-night to the last of his rustic guests. The last hour had seemed like years, and he felt, with a dim, vague consciousness, that its passage had been accompanied by the flight of something within himself that he had no power to define or to analyse. The man who now sat by the dying fire was not the man who had entered the room an hour previously. All his life had flowed with smooth purpose to that point, and there it had encountered new forces and had become—what? He tried to think what the events of the evening meant to him, but could decide nothing. All he knew was that he loved Elisabeth with a keen, strong, passionate devotion, and that her confidence in him had intensified that devotion ten-fold.

He sat while the fire died out and the parlour filled with gloom, still thinking. He recalled her voice, her manner, her attitude as she told him her story; he re-lived the moment when she burst into tears and he himself was seized with a fierce desire to take her into his arms and bid her sob out her sorrow on his breast. He had never loved her so much as at that moment, and he began to wonder why. But while he wondered, it never occurred to him that it was because of his great pity for her. He was unskilled in analysis of motive and character, despite his moody brooding over his own heart, and he had no thought within him of the foundations of his own love. It was enough for him that his heart had gone out to this particular woman.

Hepworth suddenly recalled the words which Elisabeth had spoken as she left the room. She had wished—for his sake—that she could do what he asked: he wondered if that meant that she would have married him if she had been free. He leaped at the notion as a drowning man at a passing straw. If she had been free?—might it not be that she was free? She had said that her husband might be alive or might be dead, and that if she only knew him to be dead, her mind would be at ease. And if her mind were at ease, why should she not eventually love him, Hepworth? He strode about the room, thinking it over, and at last went to bed, hopeful with new ideas. It seemed to him that his love was so great that nothing could stand in its way.

Upon the following day Hepworth detained Elisabeth in the parlour and spoke to her on the matter. He said that he was loth to re-open a subject so painful to her, but he had thought over her story and had come to the conclusion that it would be well for her peace of mind if she found out whether her husband were alive or dead.

"To live in doubt," he said, "must be terrible, Elisabeth; you said so, yourself, last night."

"Yes, sir," she answered; "but then I live in hope, too."

"Ah!" he said, "you are hoping that he will come back to you?"

"Yes," she said. "Yes—I am. But—oh! I'm afraid it's no use."

"Then why not find out all that you can?" he asked.

"I'm afraid to hear that—that he was killed," she said, "Sometimes I have a feeling that I shall see him again, and it gets so strong that I feel quite happy, and even light-hearted. And yet—I'm sure it's only because I wish that it could be so."

"Would it not be better for your peace of mind if you knew the worst or the best?" he said.

"The worst or the best?" she repeated. "Yes, sir, perhaps it would. But, oh! what if it's the worst, Mr. Hepworth, what if it's the worst?"

Hepworth said no more of the matter at that time, but after some days Elisabeth referred to it, and told him that she had been thinking it over, and had decided that it would be well to gain definite news if possible. Hepworth was secretly pleased that she should come to this decision. He felt that it might make matters plainer between them. After talking the matter over with Elisabeth, he wrote on her behalf to the governor of the convict prison in which her husband had been confined, and asked him for full information as to Verrell's fate.

Elisabeth passed the next few days in an anxious suspense which was fully shared in by Hepworth. At last she brought him his letters one morning with one lying uppermost which bore an official appearance. He looked from it to her face, and then gave it into her hands.

"Go away and read it," he said. "It's yours, Elisabeth. Tell me afterwards what news it contains."

Elisabeth came back after what seemed a long interval, during which he had sat staring at his untasted breakfast. He dare not lift his eyes when he heard her enter the room. She came to his side and laid the open letter before him.

"I know the worst now, sir," she said. "He is dead—there is no doubt."

She turned away and left the room. Hepworth read the letter, and knew why her voice had seemed so full of hopeless sorrow. The news it contained left no room for doubt. Elisabeth was free. He strode about the parlour thinking over it. Later he gave her the letter to keep, and from that time never mentioned it to her again.

The winter months went by, and at last the first faint tints of green appeared on the hedgerows, and spring came with new life. All that time Hepworth made no reference to his love, but at last he determined to speak once more. During the long days of winter time had gone for him with almost unobserved quickness—it dragged but yet hastened; circumstances seemed to pull it back, but love drove it forward, and at last Hepworth felt that he must speak all that was in his heart. Meeting Elisabeth one afternoon by the roadside outside the farmstead, he stopped her and asked her to marry him. "I will give all my life," he said, "to making you forget your sorrow. You shall be happy with me, Elisabeth."

She searched his face with earnest eyes, and then suddenly gave him her hand. "Yes," she said, "I can be happy with you; and I will try to love you."

Hepworth walked home with her. It seemed to him that a new world was opening with the new spring.

PART THE THIRD

THE EVE OF THE WEDDING

CHAPTER I
A HEART'S FIRST LOVE

Hepworth rode out of the narrow lane leading from the farmstead to the highroad, and began to whistle merrily as his horse struck into a canter. It was high summer, and the morning was full of lusty life. The long stretch of flat country to the eastward lay wrapped in dreamy mist that was even then slowly melting before the hot sunlight. Far away across the level land, towering high above the mist that wrapped their feet, rose the Wolds, a faint line of deep blue colour against the lighter tints of the sky beyond. In the foreground lay red-roofed farmsteads, thick woods newly clothed with fresh green, with the spires and towers of many a quiet village peeping above the belts of elm and beech that fenced them in. Hepworth saw the picture, and thanked God for its loveliness. It was in accord with his mood. That day, he thought, must needs be a day of sunlight and gladness, for it was the day before his wedding. On the morrow he was to call Elisabeth wife. On the morrow all life's sweetness was to be blended into perfect happiness for him. He had risen early that morning, for there was a long day's work before him. There were preparations to make, and important matters to attend to. It gave him a curious sense of pleasure to feel that everything that had to be done that day was in strict necessity of the coming event. There was no detail that did not bear some relation to it. Because he and Elisabeth were going away for a few days there were instructions to impart to Mally and admonitions to the foreman. Because the wedding-feast was to be held at the farm consultations were necessary, between Hepworth and the women. To every detail and arrangement he gave his own personal attention, not merely because Mally was cumbered with much serving, but because it pleased him intensely to feel that what he did was bringing him nearer to the happiness that he desired. It seemed to him that all the joy on earth, all the sweetness of life was being compressed by time into one perfect day, to which even a day like this was but a faint prelude. As he cantered through the lanes or across the meadows, there was within him a consciousness that every bird swinging on the slender hawthorn sprays, or flitting from one hedge to another, cried to him "To-morrow!" and that his horse's footfall echoed the same word.

Immediately after the day upon which Elisabeth consented to become his wife, Hepworth decided that she should forthwith leave the farmstead and take up her residence in the neighbouring village until the time for their marriage arrived. It did not please him to think that his future wife should any longer serve him in a menial capacity. This view of the case he concealed from Elisabeth: to her he said that she would no doubt have many preparations to make for her marriage, and would be in a better position to make them in rooms of her own. Elisabeth objected on the ground that she was not in a position to afford the expense. She was somewhat independent of spirit, and preferred to feel that she was not indebted to anyone, and especially to the man who was about to become her husband. To this Hepworth replied that she was already his promised wife, and that obligations between them were impossible. Everything that he had was hers, and therefore it was impossible that there could be any indebtedness between her and him. Elisabeth, woman-like, was scarcely able to follow the logic of this reasoning, but she gave in to Hepworth with an eager desire to please him in everything, and allowed him to carry out such arrangements as he desired. She was therefore presently installed with nothing to do but prepare for her marriage. Hepworth was desirous that the ceremony should take place before harvest, and they accordingly fixed upon a day towards the end of July. This gave Elisabeth three months in which to complete her preparations.

This time was to Hepworth the most delightful that he had ever known. He now approached Elisabeth on equal terms. She was no longer his servant, but his dearest and nearest friend, the woman whom he honoured and loved. She became his constant companion—there was not a day passed without a meeting between them. They explored the woods and fields together, and Elisabeth, quick to learn, became something of a proficient in the simpler arts of husbandry which Hepworth explained to her. This experience created a new bond of sympathy between them. It pleased her to feel that she was taking an interest in Hepworth's daily concerns; it gave him satisfaction to see the interest which she showed. Upon several occasions when he had an engagement to preach in some neighbouring village chapel she accompanied him to and fro. His sermons were now of a tone that harmonised with the newer colour of his life. He was full of love and compassion towards humanity; the warmth of his own heart seemed to flow out to all the world. Elisabeth marvelled as she heard him; it seemed to her that on these occasions he was carried to great heights, and spoke like the old prophets upon whose mysticism he largely fed his soul. She began to look forward to Sunday evening as the white-letter day of the week, for then there was always the whole afternoon in Hepworth's company, and the walk to some distant village later on, and later still, in the twilight hush, while the red afterglow faded in the western sky, and the last dreamy songs of the birds sounded from every coppice and hedgerow, the walk home again, and the confidential talk that seemed to bind her closer to the man of whose great love she was now assured.

It was Hepworth's nature to feel deeply in all things, and in the passion which Elisabeth had inspired within him, he arrived at a depth of emotion of which he could never have conceived himself capable, had he thought about the matter in earlier days. To him the woman of his choice became idealised. He invested her with charms, graces, and powers. She became the centre-piece of humanity—there was not a thought within him that did not turn towards her, or spring from her influence. Elisabeth found all this out with a woman's quick intuition. She was frightened at it, and yet she was pleased. Something of youth's light-heartedness was coming back to her life, and the pride and joy which fills a woman's heart when she finds that one man is ready to crown her queen of his soul began to re-assert themselves within her. Nevertheless, Hepworth's love for her made her anxious and half-afraid. It seemed too great, too deep for reality, and she was conscious that in everything it was far beyond the love she could give him in return. This grave, lonely, middle-aged man inspired her with respect, esteem, and a feeling that was full of gratitude, but not with the passion of love. The latter she knew, for it was still in her heart for the dead man whose life had been so full of tragedy. There was nothing of its full pulsations, its sweet emotions, its unashamed desire, in the feeling that she had for the man whom she was now to marry. Because of its absence she felt afraid.

Hepworth was also afraid because of his love, but his fear sprang from a different feeling. Once he had spoken of it to Elisabeth as they walked homeward one summer night from a distant village. He had been silent for some time, and she had asked him, half-playfully, of what he thought. He stopped and looked at her.

"Elisabeth," he said, taking her hand within his own, "do you know that I love you so much that I am afraid."

"Afraid?" she asked. "Of what?"

"Nay, that is what I do not know. Have you never known that feeling, Elisabeth? A sort of feeling that you are too happy—that a happiness so great cannot last? It seems to me sometimes that I am living in a dream, and that I shall wake and find that all my happiness is gone."

Elisabeth stood looking at him wonderingly. She did not altogether comprehend his meaning. But she suddenly smiled: her woman's wit suggested an answer.

"I am real enough," she said.

"Yes," he said. "You are real, Elisabeth. But even then—there, I can't explain what it is that I feel. If I were a boy perhaps I should feel light-hearted. But you see, Elisabeth, I am a man, and it seems to me that when a man loves, he loves with a passion which is terrible in its strength. Just to think—a year—nine months ago, I did not know you, and now—now—"

He broke off abruptly, and stood holding her hands and looking down at her.

"My God!" he said, suddenly. "If I were to lose you, Elisabeth; if I were to lose you."

Elisabeth was afraid of so much love. It seemed to her that it must lead to sorrow.

"Sometimes," she said, as they walked on, "I wish that you did not love me so much. Of course a woman is proud and glad that a man should think so much about her, but it is possible to think too much, and to estimate a person at too high a value, isn't it?"

"That," answered Hepworth, "is a question that I can't reply to, Elisabeth. What do I know of love, except that I love you?"

"Yes," she said, "I know you love me, and I like to know it—it pleases me. But I'm not sure that I like you to love me as you do, because I think I shall disappoint you. You do see what I mean, don't you? Perhaps, I can't express it properly, but I mean that if you have such a high opinion of me you are bound to be disappointed."

"I don't think I ever think of anything like that," he replied. "Love, I should think, doesn't allow people to calculate as to future events. It's just enough for me to know that of all women in the world you are the one to whom my heart goes out, and that therefore I am bound to exalt you into everything that seems perfect."

Elisabeth sighed.

"That's nice," she said, musingly. "A woman can't help liking to be told things like that. But, you know, it makes me anxious lest I shouldn't come up to the standard that's in your mind."

"I don't know how it may be," Hepworth answered. "I know so little of these things, but it seems to me that that's impossible. Perhaps love is a dream, and a dream from which one never wakes. Let us never be awakened, Elisabeth."

"I will try to make you happy," she said, suddenly turning to him. "Such love as yours deserves love in return."

But she knew beyond doubt that the fierce passionate love within him found no answering echo in her own breast, and therefore she was afraid. She wondered as she walked by his side if she would ever come to love him with the same devotion which he showed towards her. It might be, in time, she thought; and with the thought she comforted herself. Her life seemed identified with this man's: they had met in the strangest fashion: it could not be that blind fate had thrown them together for aught but good purpose. Elisabeth was somewhat fatalistic in her notions—it appeared to her that she had purposely been led to Hepworth, and with this reflection she comforted herself for the future.

So the summer passed on and now the day of the wedding was close at hand, and Hepworth rode across the smiling meadows thinking of the morrow.

CHAPTER II
ANTICIPATIONS

It was nearly noon when Hepworth rode up to his door and entered the house. In the kitchen he found Mally, who was so full of work that she had been obliged, sorely against her will, to engage the services of a couple of women from the village. These she was rating soundly when Hepworth entered, one because she was slow and lacking in comprehension, the other for her tendency to stand gossiping instead of going forward with her appointed task.

"Thank the Lord 'at weddin's doesn't come ivery day!" cried Mally, catching sight of Hepworth as he strode into the kitchen. "I used to wish 'at t' maister wod get wed, but I'm not so sure 'at I wor reight i' wishin' it. At ony rate I wish he'd waited till I wor i' my grave and i' peace. Sich a tewin' and a bustlin' as I've had this last fortnit's enow to mak' a saint sweer. And them two women—idle hussies 'at does nowt but talk and stand about and hinder a body 'at's trying to do summut! Eighteenpence a day, and their meat, and a pint o' ale to their dinners—aye, marry, I wonder what they'll ax next! Theer's ivery room i' t' house to sweep and dust, and me throng as Throp's wife and doesn't knaw which way to turn—and theer ye are, maister, come to get in t' way, I reckon."

"I shan't be here long, Mally," said Hepworth. "I want a bit of dinner and then I'm off to Sicaster, out of your way."

"Ye mud as weel ha' gone into Sicaster for your dinner," said Mally. "It's a poor time for dinners wi' t' house turned upside down and a couple o' bone-idle women i' t' road."

"Well, a bit of bread-and-cheese'll do, Mally," he answered. "Anything—I'm not particular."

"No," said Mally, contemptuously. "I reckon not. That's how men talk. Owt'll do, of course. Now then go in and sit you down, out o' t' way, and t' dinner'll be ready i' ten minutes."

Hepworth laughed and left the kitchen. But instead of going into the parlour as the old woman bade him, he passed through the house and taking a key from his pocket unlocked the door of a room looking out upon the garden and the paddock. The blinds were drawn over the old-fashioned windows, and he went across and drew them up and then turned and looked about him. He hummed a tune as he looked, and presently began to stride up and down, eyeing first one object and then another and still humming merrily.

Until recently the room in which Hepworth stood had never been in use. The old-fashioned life which he and his mother lived required no more accommodation than the parlour and the kitchen could give. During his solitary life Hepworth made the parlour his constant abiding-place, eating, reading, and thinking there with no feeling of sameness or monotony. Meanwhile the room in which he now stood became damp and musty. For months it was never opened, Mally's conception of her duty with regard to it being to sweep it out twice a-year at the spring and autumn cleanings. As a bachelor Hepworth would never have dreamed of using it, but when his marriage was arranged he made up his mind to furnish it as a best parlour for his wife. He now stood looking at the result of this decision. Hepworth intended this room as a surprise for Elisabeth. Although she had visited the house on various occasions, after leaving it for the village, Hepworth and Mally carefully contrived that she should never see the spare parlour. Once or twice there was some difficulty in preventing her from finding out that something uncommon was going on. The room had been given over to painters and paper-hangers, and later on to the furniture dealer, and the presence of these people being likely to give rise to considerable suspicion, Hepworth and Mally were more than once sorely put to it to keep the evidences of their conspiracy out of Elisabeth's sight. These difficulties, however, were now surmounted and the room was ready for its mistress. Hepworth took much pride in it, for he had spared no expense and allowed the furniture dealer to do what he pleased. Moreover, though he was not at all sure that Elisabeth could perform upon it, he had bought a piano for her. This seemed to him the crowning glory of the room, and he pictured to himself his wife's delight when she saw it.

Mally came to his side as he stood at the parlour door, silently enjoying all this splendour. She had never been within the room herself; to her it was as a holy of holies to an awestruck pilgrim. Her enjoyment of its wonders was confined to occasional peeps through the niches of the door or the window. She now stood wiping her hands, fresh from the wash-bowl, on her hard linen apron, while she gazed admiringly at the vision within.

"Now then, Mally," asked Hepworth for the twentieth time, "how does it look?"

"Varry nice, maister," said Mally. "It's fit for t' Queen to sit in. Eh, dear, I dooänt know howiver it's to be cleäned up! It'll tak' a deeäl o' dustin', and I shall be afraid o' touching ony o' t' chiny things. Aye, it's varry fine."

"You think it looks well, eh, Mally?"

"Aye, I do!" answered Mally. "Of course theer is things 'at isn't to my taste. If it hed been me, I should ha' hed summut smarter for t' wall paper—summut wi' some blue and yaller and pink in it, and happen a big flowered pattern, insteeäd o' that plain paper."

"Aye, but they tell me that this style's all the fashion now-a-days, Mally," said Hepworth. "Everything's plain and simple—so the paper-hanger said. We must be in the fashion, you know."

"Aye," answered Mally. "I expect we mun. There's nowt like being a bit fashionable."

Hepworth locked the parlour door and went to eat his dinner. Pleasant reflections came to him. He was smiling when Mally came in carrying a jug of ale.

"Just to think, Mally!" he said. "This is the last time I shall ever eat my dinner as a bachelor. Isn't that queer? The last time, Mally, the last time! I shall be married and done for to-morrow at this time."

"It's a varry serious thing, maister," said Mally. "I should ha' hed my say agen it if I didn't think t' lass 'ud mak' ye a good wife."

"She will, Mally, she will!" cried Hepworth.

"I'm sewer on it, maister. There's nowt escäpes me," said Mally. "But ye know ye mooänt forget t' owd woman 'at's slaved and tewed for ye iver sin' ye wor a lad. Owd Mally mooänt be forgotten."

She placed the jug of ale on the table with hands that trembled somewhat. Hepworth looked up at her quickly. The old woman's bright blue eye twinkled with an unshed tear, and round the wrinkles of the grim mouth there ran a sudden quiver of emotion. Hepworth suddenly comprehended matters.

"Mally, Mally!" he cried. "How can you say such things? As if I could ever forget you! Why, Mally, I look on you as the best friend I have."

"Ye'll niver find no truer," said Mally, and went away.

Presently Hepworth heard her rating the women in the kitchen. Her voice rose and fell in measured scoldings for a full five minutes.

"Poor old Mally," said Hepworth. "She's a faithful creature, and she loves me. No, I couldn't find a truer friend than Mally."

He finished his dinner and went out into the yard to order his trap to be got ready. He was going to Sicaster, and had parcels to bring back which he could not well carry in the saddle. Then he made himself smart and drove away. In the village he stopped at the gate of the cottage where Elisabeth lived. She caught sight of him through the window and came down the path to him. He bent down and looked earnestly at her. Elisabeth blushed as she met his ardent gaze.

"You are going into Sicaster?" she said.

"Yes, Elisabeth. There are two or three things I have to get, and there's my wedding finery to try on for the last time. Yours, I expect, is all ready?"

"Yes," she said, laughing. "I think it is."

Then they were silent, Hepworth watching the girl's face, and she looking away from him along the road. As he watched her he could not help contrasting the Elisabeth that he now saw with the Elisabeth of the statute hiring fair. That was a sad-faced Elisabeth, a woman losing her youth and good looks under a cloud of sorrow—this was a girl again, with a happy face and bright eyes and a look of hopefulness.

"You are looking well to-day, Elisabeth," said Hepworth presently. "Against an old fellow like me you look quite a girl. You are getting really beautiful."

Elisabeth smiled as she turned to him.

"Am I?" she said. "Then I am glad for your sake. I want to make you happy."

"No fear of my happiness," he said. "My dear—my dear—I am the happiest man alive, I think! Good-bye, Elisabeth—I shall see you to-night, and that, please God, will be our last parting. Good-bye, my dear, good-bye."

He drove away, and Elisabeth, standing at the garden gate, watched him out of sight. He turned at the bend of the highway and waved his hand and so went onward.

Hepworth, on arriving at Sicaster, stabled his horse at the inn and then pursued his business. He had numerous calls to make, and at each place he found himself compelled to receive congratulations on the approaching event. Everybody seemed to derive some satisfaction from the thought that Hepworth was to be married.

"A very joyful occasion this, sir," said the little tailor who fitted on the wedding coat. "Very joyful indeed, if I may be allowed to say so. A very proper figure of a man you do make in that coat, Mr. Hepworth. Your good lady, sir, will be proud of you."

Hepworth laughed and went away to the inn. He had finished all his business then and turned into the bar-parlour to smoke a pipe before driving home. The bar-parlour already had several occupants. Two or three farmers of Hepworth's acquaintance sat there, together with a butcher and a cattle-dealer with whom they had evidently been doing business. In a corner near the fire-place sat a young man, apparently a stranger to the rest of the company.

Hepworth's arrival was greeted with a round of applause. The oldest of the men rose to his feet and insisted on shaking him by the hand.

"Dang it!" said he. "It's a long lane 'at hes no turnin', and I allus said 'at he'd wed some day or another. Here's good luck, my lad."

"Thank you," said Hepworth. "I'm heartily obliged to you."

"It's a joyful occasion is a weddin'," said the old farmer. "Eh, I mind mine as weel as if it wor yesterday! It's nigh on to forty year sin', but it's fresh enew i' my memory. Aye, so it is."

"I think Mestur Hepworth mun ax us to drink his wife's health," said the drover, with a roguish twinkle of the eye. "It's t' least we can do on such a joyful occasion. I've drunk a many healths i' my time, but niver one 'at I'd drink wi' more pleasure."

"Nor me," said the butcher. "I allus had a great respect for Mr. Hepworth."

"I shall be very glad, friends," said Hepworth. "It's very kind of you. Perhaps the young lady 'll take the company's orders. What'll you all take, gentlemen?"

The men named their drinks to the young woman behind the bar. Hepworth turned to the stranger in the corner. He felt ready to treat a whole room full of people and to ask them to drink to his happiness.

"Will you join us, sir?" he said politely. "I shall be very much honoured."

"Thank you, sir," answered the stranger. "The honour is mine, I'm sure."

When the glasses had been handed round the old farmer rose to his feet and held his up.

"Here's to the health—" he began. "Come," he said, pausing—"I don't know t' young lady's name. Give us her name, Hepworth, lad—all friends here, you know."

"Mrs. Elisabeth Verrell," said Hepworth.

"Then here's to Mrs. Elisabeth Verrell, Mrs. Hepworth as is to be—long life and much joy to her and her good man," said the old farmer.

The others re-echoed the sentiment and drained their glasses to the bottom, setting them on the table with a hearty ring. But when the stranger caught the name he suddenly sat down in the seat from which he had risen and put his glass on the table untasted.

The stranger . . . sat down in the seat from which he had risen.

CHAPTER III
THE BLOW FALLS

During the next half-hour the men assembled in the bar-parlour of the inn continued to smoke, drink, and chat. The old farmer was somewhat inclined to tease Hepworth about his marriage, and threw out sundry sly hints as to the sudden frivolities of middle-aged men. Hepworth took all in good part: he was so heartily at peace with himself and all the world that nothing could ruffle the calm sea of his content. He smoked his pipe and laughed at the old man's humour. Half of what was said he did not hear—he was thinking of Elisabeth. Once or twice, glancing round the room he caught sight of the stranger in the corner. The young man still sat with his glass untasted before him. He kept his eyes fixed on Hepworth, and seemed to be studying him with a curious interest. Hepworth, however, scarcely noted it—all that day he had been thinking of the morrow, and no other thought had power to turn him from it. He was so absorbed that he did not even notice that the stranger had not tasted the contents of the glass before him. At last Hepworth shook the ashes out of his pipe and rose to go. The old farmer would have detained him on the plea of drinking another glass. Hepworth declined laughingly. The company then insisted upon his shaking hands with them individually. They pressed his hand with much fervour, wishing him joy. While this ceremony was going on the stranger rose and left the room.

In the inn-yard the ostler was yoking Hepworth's horse. Hepworth came out and began counting the parcels under the seat of the trap, to make sure that all were there, and none missing. While he was thus engaged, the stranger came up.

"Can I speak to you a minute?" he said, addressing Hepworth.

Hepworth looked round in some astonishment. It occurred to him that the young man might be a hawker, selling something and anxious to trade with him.

"Yes, certainly," he replied, "but I'm afraid I haven't much time."

"Let us go into the inn—into some private room," said the stranger.

"Eh?" said Hepworth. "A private room? Why?"

"So that we can talk without interruption. What I wish to say to you is of a private nature."

"I don't understand you," said Hepworth.

"I want to speak to you on important matters, then," said the stranger.

Hepworth re-arranged his parcels, wondering what the man meant. He was impatient to drive away, so that he might get home early and spend an hour with Elisabeth.

"Can't you say what you want to say here?" he asked. "You see—I'm in a hurry."

"No," answered the stranger. "Come into the inn. I must speak to you—do you hear—must! It's a matter of great importance—it's about—about your marriage."

Hepworth turned and looked at the stranger in astonishment. He then perceived that the young man was much agitated, and that something of moment had occurred. He called to the ostler and bidding him see to the horse, led the way into the house again.

"Let it be a private room," said the young man.

Hepworth opened the door of a small parlour at the end of a passage, and motioning the stranger to enter, followed him and closed it carefully behind them.

Then he turned to him. The young man sank down into a chair and seemed to be labouring under some emotion. He rested his head on his hand and looked at Hepworth with frightened eyes.

"Well?" said Hepworth.

"I'm forced to speak," said the stranger. "It's all chance that I should have come here this afternoon and met you. A day later, and the chance would have gone."

"What do you want to say?" Hepworth asked.

"You were to be married to-morrow to a young woman named Elisabeth Verrell?"

"Were to be? I am to be—what of it?"

"You cannot marry her."

Hepworth looked at him silently. He felt as if he were dreaming: there was something unreal about the whole thing. He seemed to be no longer himself but rather another man looking on at his own doings, hearing his own words.

"Cannot?" he said at last, after what appeared to him a long silence. "And why?"

"Because, sir, she is already married."

"That," said Hepworth, "I know. But her husband is dead—she is a widow."

"No, sir. Her husband lives."

At these words Hepworth suddenly regained full consciousness of his own being. He felt a fierce throb of anguish that made him stagger and turn sick. He sat down in the nearest chair and looked earnestly at the stranger.

"Proof of it!" he said. "Proof, man—for God's sake!"

The stranger sank his voice to a whisper.

"I trust to you," he said. "You must be an honest man, or Elisabeth—well, then, I am her husband—I am Walter Verrell."

For some five minutes after that the two men sat facing each other, their eyes staring, their faces white and drawn. Hepworth felt that all was over. He knew it was true. Something told him that this was no ugly dream, but an uglier reality. It was all over—and his great love was doomed to come to naught. He tried to think, but thought would not come to him. All he was conscious of was that something had struck him to the heart and numbed his life.

Presently, Hepworth rose and went over to the window and looked out. In the yard stood his horse and trap, with two or three stable-boys lounging near it; through the gate of the inn he saw people pass to and fro about the market-place, bright and pleasant in the light of the afternoon sun; the laughter of a child in a neighbouring garden came to his ears. He noted all these things with a strange sense of keenness—they seemed to burn themselves into his brain.

"She told me you were dead," he said, suddenly turning to his companion. "Dead!"

"She does not know that I am not," answered Verrell. "I—do you know my story?"

"Yes," said Hepworth. "Yes—yes—I know."

"They thought I was dead—shot—and I saw in the papers that they found my body. It was not mine—I escaped."

Hepworth continued to stare out of the window. He was not yet able to think clearly over what had happened. Once more he began to fancy that it was a dream. It must be a dream—he was asleep of course, in his bed at the farm, and presently Mally would come knocking at his door and he would wake to find the sunlight pouring in through the window, and—

"What is to be done?" asked Verrell.

Hepworth started. Done? Then it was no dream. To do something meant action, reality. It was no dream.

"Done?" he said. "Done? I don't know—I can't think. Of course you are right—there is something to be done. But what? I can't think yet—give me time."

He spoke in disconnected sentences, feeling that he was not master of himself. Try as he would he could not think—it seemed to him that the blow which had just fallen upon him had numbed his faculties and rendered him wholly incapable of thought. It was difficult to speak, but more difficult to think.

"I suppose we must do something," he said at last, his voice full of despair. "It is all over, of course." He sat down and looked at Verrell.

"We must tell Elisabeth—your wife," he said. "After that—"

He paused, not knowing what to say next. Verrell said nothing. He sat silently watching Hepworth.

"How did you come here?" asked Hepworth, wearily.

Verrell leaned forward and spoke in a low voice. His eyes wandered to the door, then to the window, as if he dreaded to be overheard.

"It's a long story," he said. "A long story, Mr. Hepworth. You know that I have been in prison—Elisabeth told you, no doubt."

"Yes," said Hepworth. "Yes—she told me."

His mind went back to the night on which Elisabeth had told the story of her sorrow to him. He saw her weeping again, and again felt the wild desire that then filled him to take her into his arms and comfort her. While Verrell spoke, this picture remained before Hepworth's eyes. He saw Elisabeth and her grief, and began to wonder whether she then felt as he was feeling now.

"I escaped from prison," said Verrell, glancing nervously around him. "It was a marvellous escape, too. I met a man on Dartmoor whom I took into my confidence. He promised to assist me. We were hid all one day, and at night we crossed the moors. It was moonlight, and there was a search party out, and they saw us and shot at us from a distance. The man was hit. I dragged him into a sort of cave in a lonely spot. Then he died, and it seemed to me that there was a chance of escape. I took his clothes off and put them on myself, and left my clothes—the prison clothes—on him. Then I went away. They found him a long time after—and of course they thought it was the escaped convict. He—he was unrecognisable, but there were the clothes to go by."

"And after that?" said Hepworth.

"I got down to Plymouth," continued Verrell. "There was money in the dead man's clothes, and I purchased a new outfit as soon as possible, and burnt his clothes lest anyone should recognise them. Then I went to sea in a ship bound for South America. I was out there sometime, but I came home at last because—because of Elisabeth. I ventured to go to Bristol and enquire after her, and then I tracked her to Clothford, and at Clothford I found the woman with whom she had worked, and learned that she was in your service. That's how I came here to-day. It was just chance that made us meet."

"Chance?" said Hepworth. "Chance?"

He began to laugh—Verrell shuddered to hear it; it was such soulless, despairing laughter. Suddenly Hepworth shook himself and turned to the door.

"Come!" he said. "No more talking—we must go."

CHAPTER IV
HEPWORTH'S QUESTION

"Where are you going?" asked Verrell, following Hepworth from the parlour and down the passage to the door. There was something in Hepworth's voice and manner that alarmed him. Hepworth stood at the door, staring absently-minded at his horse and trap. At Verrell's question he laughed harshly and turned to look at his questioner with a strange expression on his face.

"Aye, where?" said he. "Where? Come, we must go somewhere. There is much to do, and the sooner we set about doing it the better."

Verrell followed him to the trap. Hepworth bade him get in and took the reins from the ostler. He drove out of the yard by the back entrance.

"Look here," said Verrell, "I don't know where you're taking me, but I hope it is not through the town. I want to escape observation as much as possible, you know, because—"

"Afraid of being caught, eh?" said Hepworth, and began to laugh again.

"You never know who there may be watching you," said Verrell, nervously. He wished Hepworth would not laugh in so strange a fashion. It seemed to him that it was the laughter of a madman. He glanced at Hepworth's face, and was still more uneasy. It was white and drawn as if with intense pain and there was a look in his eyes that frightened Verrell as much as the harsh, soulless laughter.

"We're going home," said Hepworth presently. "And we'll go by a quiet road. You need not be afraid. There's nobody will know you—it's most likely that we shan't meet a soul all the way."

"And when we get home," asked Verrell, "what shall we do? Is—is Elisabeth at your house now?"

"No," answered Hepworth.

"I suppose I had better see her at once!" said Verrell. "Of course, you will have to tell her that the marriage cannot take place."

Hepworth set his teeth firmly together, and brought down the whip in his right hand with savage force across the horse's flanks. The horse started violently and then plunged forward. Hepworth tightened his hold on the reins, and laughed again. Verrell shivered and clutched at the seat.

"It frightens me," he said, "to hear you laugh like that."

"You think I'm mad," said Hepworth bluntly, "I know you do.

Well, perhaps I am. I think I went mad when I found out who you are."

"I am sorry," said Verrell. "Very sorry. I wish it could have been different. I've known sorrow, too, and so has my wife. I suppose you love her—"

"Man alive!" cried Hepworth. "Do you want to drive me mad altogether? Don't you see that it's almost killing me, this awful thing? Love her? My God, man, what do you know about love? You're young, you're a boy—look at me, I'm middle-aged, old, if you like, and I never loved in my life until I saw her. And now we're to be parted."

"Think of what it must have been when we were parted," said Verrell, quietly.

Hepworth nodded his head. He remembered the agony which Elisabeth had shown when she told him her story.

"I can't think," he answered. "I know what it must have been, but I can't think. The blow has broken me, man, I feel as if I were dead—dead as a door-nail and yet more alive than ever I was. That's what it must be to be in hell. I am in hell, Verrell—yes, in hell."

He drove on in silence. Instead of taking the high-road from Sicaster he had turned into a bye-lane through the fields, and over its ruts and uneven surface he drove swiftly forward, occasionally urging the horse on with blows of the whip. The trap rocked from side to side, and Verrell was obliged to hold on to keep his seat, but Hepworth paid no heed. A long, trailing branch from an overhanging tree caught his face and tore the skin and drew blood, but he gave no sign. Coming at last to a turn in the lane which brought them within sight of the woods beyond which lay the farmstead, he drew rein, and brought the sweating horse to a walking pace.

"What are your plans?" he said curtly.

"Plans?"

"You've some notion of what you're going to do, I suppose," said Hepworth. "You didn't come here for nothing."

"I came to find my wife," answered Verrell.

"Well, now you know where she is, what are you going to do? You'll go away with her, I expect."

"Yes," said Verrell. "I expect so. You see I haven't any definite plans, because I didn't know where Elisabeth might be. Now that I have found her I suppose we must go quietly away and hide ourselves—perhaps in America."

"Have you any money?" asked Hepworth bluntly.

"Not much," answered Verrell.

Hepworth pulled up his horse. The trap stood under the shadow of a grove of trees just where the lane crossed the great highway. Hepworth pointed across the lane with his whip.

"Get out," he said. "Go into those trees—you'll find a sort of hut in the middle, and you can stay there for a while until I bring your wife. It may be two or three hours yet. You must wait."

"Yes," said Verrell. He got out and advanced towards the trees.

"Stop a bit," said Hepworth, suddenly recalling him. He leaned over the side of the trap and looked Verrell searchingly in the face. "I know your story," he said. "Your wife thinks you were innocent. Tell me the truth. Before God—were you innocent?"

Verrell hung his head. For a moment he said nothing. Then he looked up and answered in a low voice, "No, I was not!"

Hepworth withdrew his eyes slowly from Verrell's upturned face. He was about to speak, but he suddenly shook the reins and drove away along the lane.

CHAPTER V
TEMPTATION

Before he came to the point where the bye-way turned down through the woods to his farmstead, Hepworth let the reins drop on his horse's back and began to think. Verrell's admission had acted upon him like a sudden douche of ice-cold water. He was himself again, and felt prepared to think and act after his ordinary level-headed fashion. The sorrow that had come to him was still with him, but it no longer bore him down with a fierce regret that was half-madness. He now felt that it must be grappled with and conquered for Elisabeth's sake. So far he had thought only of himself; since Verrell's admission of his guilt he had begun to think for the woman he loved.

The horse, wearied and frightened by the harsh treatment it had received, dropped into a slow walk, hanging its head and panting. Hepworth let it go its own way. He sat with folded arms and bowed head, thinking gloomily.

"All is over," he said to himself. "I have lived in a fool's paradise, and now I am turned out of it. I used to wonder at Elisabeth when she first told me of her doubts about God, but now I half believe in what she said. What a mockery is life! Here am I, loving with all my heart a woman who is tied to another man. She loved that man passionately once, and believed in him with absolute confidence, and all the time he was deceiving her. She and I would have been happy together—it couldn't have been otherwise, because I love her. And now it's all over—and I'm sick at heart for wonder that God lets such things be. Oh, I don't wonder that Elisabeth had doubts. It seems as if God played shuttlecock with human lives. Is there a God? Once I never doubted it—I was content then. Did I ever think? I don't know—contented folk never ask themselves the why or wherefore of anything."

So he went on, thinking sombrely of his trouble, until the horse came to the gate of the narrow way that led to the farmstead. There he pulled himself together and took up the reins and drove at a quicker pace to the door of the house. He got out of the trap and collected his parcels and walked steadily into the kitchen. It was then six o'clock, and Mally and the two women were having a cup of tea at the table in the window-place. Mally looked at her master with some curiosity.

"Massy on us!" she said; "ye're lookin' badly, maister—that white and drawn. Aren't you weel?"

"I'm all right," he answered. "It's very hot to-day—it's the heat,

Mally."

"I'll mak' you a cup o' fresh tea at once," said Mally. "It's varry coolin' is tea—nowt like it i' summer."

"No," he said, "I don't want it. I don't want anything just now, Mally—let me be."

He walked into the parlour and flung his parcels upon the table, and sat down in his chair with a sigh. He remembered with what joy and animation he had gone out of that room only a few hours previously. Then he felt a young man, instinct with life and vigour; now there was a curious, vague feeling of old age about him—it seemed to him that he had aged suddenly.

He sat for some minutes thinking in this way. One of his men came along the yard and took away the horse and trap; a child passed the window carrying a milk-jug. He noted these things with that keen appreciation which comes over the mind in times of pain or sorrow. At last he turned from the window and rose, walking aimlessly across the floor. A half-open drawer in the bureau in which he kept his papers attracted his attention. He laid his hand on it, intending to close it, but in the act his eyes became riveted to an object lying within. He stood, with the drawer half-closed, staring at the thing before him. The object at which Hepworth gazed was a revolver, the polished butt of which was partly covered by a loose mass of papers.

A full minute went by, and still Hepworth stood and stared fixedly at the thing which had caught his eye. He suddenly picked it up and went back to the chair from which he had lately risen, and sitting down, looked at it. He had bought it years before, in order to protect himself when coming home late along the lonely roads, but he had never used it, though it had been kept clean and bright against need to carry it. He examined it carefully now, and noticed that the chambers were all charged, and that everything was in proper order.

Hepworth began to think. With the power that lay concealed within those shining chambers he could cut the knot that now tied up all the sweet possibilities of life. Verrell was in that lonely grove of trees, absolutely alone, and not a soul in the world knew of his presence there. He was a man already believed to be dead. The law recognised him as dead. He had no friends to enquire for him. The people who saw him drive away with Hepworth from Sicaster would never ask after him, for they knew nothing about him. How easy to destroy him, to hide his body, and thus to put an end to the difficulties which his life raised in Hepworth's path!

Hepworth rose and went over to the sideboard and poured himself out a stiff glass of whisky from the decanter that stood there. He drank it at a gulp, and sat down again, and played with the revolver and continued to think.

How easy to do it! And why not? Why should he fear? There was no God! God could not play fast and loose with human hearts, and since human hearts were played with in this fashion there was no God. There was naught but blind fate, cold, cruel, merciless. Let him defy it—let him take the power that life gave him into his own hands and conquer everything by sheer strength of will and purpose. Since everything was against him, let him be against everything. Fate had been kind in one way: it had shown him a means of removing from his path its only obstacle without a fear of discovery.

Hepworth rose. He slipped the revolver into his pocket, and leaving the parlour passed through the porch into the garden and went round the corner of the house, intending to walk across the fields to the spot where he had left Verrell. But before he turned out of the garden he passed an open window and heard voices in the room within. A chance word made him pause and then shrink close to the wall and listen.

Mally and one of the women were talking. They had forgotten their differences in their desire to gossip, and they now conversed as they swept and dusted.

"Dosta think shoo'll mak' t' maister a good wife, then?" said the woman.

"Aye, I think shoo will," said Mally. "I tuke a deeäl o' notice on her when shoo wor here, and shoo seemed a nice, tidy, weel-be-haäved young woman."

"I wonder if shoo thinks a deeäl on 'im."

"That's more nor I can say," answered Mally. "Tha sees, lass, shoo'd been wed afore. Aye, and seemed to think a deeäll aboot her first husband! Theer wor one neet, at efter shoo'd promised to wed t' maister 'at I see'd her wi' her first husband's pictur—eh, dear, poor thing, shoo wor crying over it like a babby. Shoo kissed it, and hugged it to her, and then she'd luke at it for iver soa long, and kiss it ageeän. Soöa tho sees, mi lass, hahiver much shoo may think o' t' new, shoo hasn't forgat t' owd 'un; noäa, and niver will, and if he wor to rise throo' t' grave shoo'd göa to him, chuse what! Theer niver wor a woman i' this world 'at forgat her first love."

Hepworth walked quietly away. He turned out of the garden by a door that led into the fold. The fold was quiet; the men were in the back-kitchen at supper; everything lay hushed and peaceful under the summer evening's calm.

There was a well in one corner of the fold, covered by a stout oaken lid, raised by a heavy iron ring. He bent over and lifted the lid, and feeling for the revolver drew it from his pocket and dropped it into the well. He heard it splash far below. The noise of the falling lid drowned the echoes of the splash.

Hepworth turned back to the house. He went into the parlour and unlocked a small safe that stood in the cupboard. From an inner drawer he took out a pocket-book, and having put this in his breast, he left the house and walked swiftly towards the village.

Verrell found himself gazing at his wife.

CHAPTER VI
WHERE HIGHWAYS CROSS

It was the middle of the evening when Hepworth reached the cottage in which Elisabeth lived. The old woman who kept it was standing at the garden gate as he approached.

"Shoo's gone out," she said, before Hepworth could speak.

Hepworth paused, his hand on the gate-latch.

"Where?" he said.

"Naay, maister, I doön't know. Shoo sed it wor a grand evenin', and shoo'd hev a bit on a walk. Shoo thowt ye wadn't be comin' so soon, happen."

"Which way did she go?" he asked.

"Shoo went up t' hill yonder," answered the old woman. "I see'd her crossin' t' fields hafe-an-hour agöa."

Hepworth went away in the direction indicated. The path which the old woman pointed out to him led towards the grove of trees where he had left Verrell.

Elisabeth had been busied within the house for the greater part of the day, concluding her preparations for her wedding. Towards evening she felt that a breath of fresh air would do her good, and she accordingly took her hat and went out, intending to be home again within the hour. She knew that Hepworth would come to see her that night, but she did not expect him before eight or nine o'clock. Once out of doors she went further than she had intended. The evening air was cool and delicious to breathe; birds were singing in every hedgerow and coppice, and the laughter of the village children rang in subdued cadences up the low hillsides. She walked on and on, and ere long came to the grove of trees where Hepworth and Verrell had parted.

Verrell, after watching Hepworth drive away, went into the grove and looked for the hut. He found it in the centre of a clearing—a rude, decaying structure of pine-logs, with a thatched roof, gradually falling into ruin and wreck. He went in, and finding it cold and comfortless left it and sat outside on a fallen tree. The place was quiet—there seemed to be no life near it other than that of the birds and insects that sang and hummed in the undergrowth. He brought out a pipe and tobacco and began to smoke. When one pipe was finished he filled another. For two hours he sat there, smoking and thinking, and listening for the sound of a footstep on the dry brushwood.

At last a sound, the cracking of a broken twig pressed by a human foot, reached him. With the instinct of quick fear he left the fallen tree and made for the hut, hiding himself in its darkest corner. Through a window destitute of glass, he peered into the trees without. The sound came nearer; suddenly the thick-leaved branches were pushed aside, and a woman stepped into the clearing. Verrell found himself gazing at his wife.

Elisabeth had often visited this spot. In spring she went there to seek primroses; in summer she sought its privacy in order to think quietly over the new departure in her life. Finding herself near the grove of trees that night she had turned in there for half-an-hour's quiet thought. When Verrell saw her he concluded that Hepworth had sent her to find him, but he almost immediately perceived that in this supposition he was mistaken. Elisabeth sat down on the fallen tree, almost on the spot he had just left, and he saw that she believed herself to be quite alone and unobserved.

Verrell remained at the window watching his wife. Elisabeth sat, thoughtful and quiet, her hands folded idly in her lap, her eyes fixed on the ground. She was evidently deep in thought. He noticed that she was graver than he remembered her, and that a certain womanly dignity had replaced the girlish light-hearted air that he had never forgotten. A curious feeling of wonder came over him as he looked at her. It seemed to him that she was the same, yet not the same.

Presently Elisabeth drew something from her pocket and looked at it long and thoughtfully. A turn of her hand showed Verrell that it was his own photograph. "She is thinking of me," he said to himself, and at the thought his eyes filled with tears and a new wave of life welled up within him. Then he saw that Elisabeth was softly crying to herself. She raised the photograph to her lips and kissed it. Verrell waited no longer. He stepped to the open door of the hut.

"Elisabeth!" he said. "Elisabeth!"

Elisabeth looked up. She saw her husband standing before her. At the sight she felt herself swooning—it was a dream, she thought, a dream that must suddenly change, and yet it was burning itself into her heart and brain with a reality which no dream can possess. She rose to her feet, and stood gazing and trembling. Verrell moved swiftly towards her. "Elisabeth!" he said again.

"Walter!"

Her voice came faint and low. She held out her hands as if she were suddenly going blind and needed guidance.

"Oh," she cried, as he took her in his arms. "It is you—it is you! I thought you were dead. My dear—my dear—my dear!"

It was half-an-hour after this that Hepworth came into the grove of trees. He had looked for Elisabeth along the lanes and fields and had failed to find her. Thinking that she had returned to the village he had come to the grove to take Verrell away. But as he advanced through the undergrowth he suddenly heard people talking. He went forward cautiously and recognised the voices as those of Elisabeth and Verrell. Advancing quietly towards the clearing he came close behind them. They sat on the fallen tree, talking earnestly. Verrell's arm was about his wife's neck: she leaned against him confidently, and there was a look on her face that Hepworth had never seen there before.

Verrell had told Elisabeth all that had taken place between him and Hepworth. But he had resolved while he waited for the latter to tell her something more, and he was beginning this difficult task when Hepworth came up behind them. Hepworth caught the first words. "Elisabeth," said Verrell, "there is something that I must tell you. My dear, we have to begin our life again, and it will be hard—"

"Oh," she said, "as if I cared, now that I have got you back, Walter! We will go somewhere, far away, and we will be happy—happy, my dear, as we used to be."

"Yes," he said, "but I must tell you, dear, before we go—"

Hepworth seized the situation at a glance. Verrell was going to tell his wife that he had deceived her as to his innocence. The thought flashed rapidly through his mind—why should that confession be made? What good would it do? The expression on Elisabeth's face told him that she would forgive anything. Why should she not continue to believe in the man she loved? He suddenly stepped into the clearing. Elisabeth and Verrell started to their feet.

"So you have found each other?" said Hepworth.

The three stood looking into each other's faces. A moment that seemed a lifetime passed. Then Elisabeth, womanly-quick to see the pain in Hepworth's face, came to his side and laid her hand on his arm.

"Oh," she said, her face full of divine compassion. "I am sorry, I am so sorry. You have been so good, so kind to me. But,"—she turned to Verrell with a wonderful look of love and pride—"he is my husband."

Hepworth gave her hand a quick, strong grip.

"Yes," he said. "I know. Say no more, Elisabeth. Let your husband come with me for a minute—I must speak to him."

The two men went into the hut. Once inside Hepworth turned to Verrell.

"You were going to tell your wife that you were not innocent?" he said.

"Yes," said Verrell.

"Don't tell her," said Hepworth. "She believes in you—let her continue to believe. No one will ever be able to persuade her to the contrary. Only," here he laid his hand on the young man's shoulder, "promise me to live worthy of her!"

"I will—God help me!" said Verrell.

"Now listen," continued Hepworth. "I have thought things over for you. Here is money in this pocket-book; take it, man, take it!—there is a train leaves Sicaster in an hour for Liverpool, and you must catch it. Go by the first ship to America—do what you can there—if you ever want help, write to me."

"God bless you!" said Verrell.

"Now come outside," said Hepworth.

He went back to Elisabeth, Verrell following close behind him. Hepworth held out his hand to the woman he loved.

"Good-bye, Elisabeth," he said. "Go with your husband—he will tell you what you are to do. Good-bye—good-bye!"

She took his hand and held it. Their eyes met.

"Good-bye!" she said.

Still they held each other's hands. Verrell turned away. Hepworth felt the bitterness of death upon him as he gazed into Elisabeth's eyes.

"Good-bye!" he said again. "Good-bye, Elisabeth!"

Without another word the three went slowly through the wood and into the lane. Hepworth pointed out the road towards Sicaster and silently motioned them to take it. Elisabeth was weeping as she turned away from him. Verrell paused and held out his hand and wrung Hepworth's within it. Then he hurried on and took his wife's hand and they went along the lane in the fast-gathering twilight. Hepworth stood watching them. At the bend of the road Elisabeth turned and waved her hand to him. He lifted his own in response. The next moment they were gone, and he stood there, alone.

In this way Hepworth said farewell to the love of his life.

THE END

www.ingramcontent.com/pod-product-compliance
Lightning Source LLC
Chambersburg PA
CBHW011438170626
46808CB00009B/3096